D...
SOUND FAMILIAR?

Donna resents learning about history. She can't see how it relates to her life, so she closes her mind to the subject and refuses to learn anything.

Ricky complains about too much board work (tedious copying). He resents having to write and write and write, claiming that nothing actually registers in his brain.

William's social studies teacher likes to share his travel experiences with the class. However, he forgets himself and gets carried away talking about his wonderful memories.

Tanya's teacher has fallen into the trap of making faulty assumptions. She had a negative experience with Tanya's brother, so she assumes she will also have trouble with Tanya.

**If you can relate
to any of these problems,
MY TEACHER IS DRIVING ME CRAZY
can help!**

Also by Joyce Vedral:

I DARE YOU*
MY PARENTS ARE DRIVING ME CRAZY*
I CAN'T TAKE IT ANYMORE*
THE OPPOSITE SEX IS DRIVING ME CRAZY*
MY TEENAGER IS DRIVING ME CRAZY*
BOYFRIENDS*

Physical Fitness Titles:
NOW OR NEVER
SUPER CUT
HARD BODIES
PERFECT PARTS
THE HARD BODIES EXPRESS WORKOUT
THE 12-MINUTE TOTAL-BODY WORKOUT
THE FAT-BURNING WORKOUT

*Published by Ballantine Books

MY TEACHER IS DRIVING ME CRAZY

Joyce L. Vedral, Ph.D.

BALLANTINE BOOKS • NEW YORK

Copyright © 1991 by Joyce Vedral, Ph.D.

All rights reserved under International and Pan-American Copyright Conventions. Published in the United States of America by Ballantine Books, a division of Random House, Inc., New York, and simultaneously in Canada by Random House of Canada Limited, Toronto.

Library of Congress Catalog Card Number: 91-91978

ISBN 0-345-36648-4

Manufactured in the United States of America

First Edition: October 1991

– DEDICATION –

To the late Dory Davidson, a woman who spent her youth, her energy, indeed her life, being a giving, loving, dedicated teacher, a person who had a positive influence upon not only her students, but her colleagues as well

And to the teachers of the world—who patiently plod along, day by day, in an effort to make a difference in the lives of their students, and who are thrilled to accept as payment for their long hours and hard work the reward of changing even one life for the better

And to students everywhere, who are struggling to get an education, I offer this book as a guide to understanding teacher behavior, and as a practical manual for improving your grades

– CONTENTS –

- ACKNOWLEDGMENTS -

To the teachers of Julia Richman High School, for allowing me to interview you for this book, and because you all fall into the chapter entitled "The Wonderful Teacher."

To our warm, sensitive, devoted principal, Susan De Armas, for being there for students, parents, and teachers alike.

To Jack Valerio, Chairman of the English Department—for taking the time, for listening, and for radiating joy and love. How many times have I watched as you patiently listened as a student poured out a lengthy complaint about a class or a teacher and then observed you resolve the situation with a wisdom that can truly be called "a gift."

To George Ryan—a star teacher who asks for no reward, but quietly gives his all, and who after some twenty years can still be seen on any given day, teaching with the same enthusiasm and animation that he had the day he started.

To the teachers of high schools and junior high schools all over the United States, for allowing me to interview you and for honestly sharing your thoughts, feelings, and experiences—the negative as well as the positive.

To the students of Julia Richman High School, General Douglass MacArthur High School, and high schools and junior high schools all over the United States, for telling me about your best and worst experiences with teachers and for maintaining a sense of humor through it all.

To Oprah Winfrey, for inspiring me to write this book by her enlightening show on high school dropouts.

To Bob Wyatt, editor in chief. Every time I have had a conversation with you, I have learned. You have been my mentor for years.

To the late Richard McCoy, for your professionalism, your efficiency, your kindness and your willingness to go the extra mile. Your gentle spirit will live on forever in the lives you've touched.

To Jim Freed, for your patience, diligence, and willing assistance.

To Rick Balkin, agent and friend. I thank you for "discovering" me and for guiding my career.

To family and friends for your loving attention.

To my daughter, Marthe Simone Vedral, for reading and criticizing the manuscript and for demonstrating in high school as well as college that you have learned your lesson well. I'm proud of you.

1

My Teacher Is Driving Me Crazy

"I failed English because the teacher was boring."

"My math teacher had a nasty attitude, so I just started cutting."

"My global studies teacher works us to death. No one could get a high mark in that course."

You're a teenager, just trying to survive. You have other things on your mind besides school, but school is a big part of your life—whether you like it or not. You would like to pass all of your courses, and with the highest grades possible, but your teachers make that very difficult. They drive you crazy. If they're not being sarcastic and insulting, they're being unfair. If they're not boring you to death, they're working you to death. And if they're not working you to death, they're either letting the class walk all over them while you learn nothing, or they're sitting there reading the paper while you copy endless amounts of board work. If not any of the above, perhaps the problem is that you are forced to deal with an "eyesore" whose looks and smell are enough to sink a battleship, or at least to tempt you beyond your limit to cut class. But whatever the problem is, the fact is: You feel like you've had it with school.

If your teacher is driving you crazy, if you've ever had a teacher that has driven you crazy, or, if you want to find out how to deal with teachers who may try to drive you crazy in the future, this book is for you.

-THE GOAL OF THIS BOOK-

The goal of this book is not to put teachers down. The large majority of teachers are wonderful people. In fact, I think just about all of them are—only, being human, they have faults. The purpose of this book is to show you how to survive situations in which something about your teacher bothers you or upsets you—or *everything* bothers you and you simply can't stand the teacher!

You don't have to fail that course or accept a low grade anymore. Instead you can pass with a higher mark than you ever imagined. How? By gaining insight into why teachers behave the way they do, and then by learning exactly how to deal with each specific "problem" teacher. No longer do you have to throw up your hands and say, "Forget about it. It's hopeless. I'll just have to make this up in summer school."

-WHAT YOU WILL FIND IN THIS BOOK-

In chapters one and two, you'll find out why teachers become teachers in the first place. You'll discover why they keep on teaching in spite of the fact that they are underpaid and overworked. You'll learn how difficult it is to be a teacher, and you'll find out the secret things that teachers have to put up with from their bosses—the department chairperson, the assistant principal, and the principal. You'll discover why some teachers live in fear of being "written up," and why other teachers rebel and refuse to do clerical work, patrol halls, or punch in on time clocks. You'll learn about how teachers sometimes report each other in order to get each other in trouble—or keep themselves out of it. You'll find out what teachers go through in their personal lives, and why they usually keep it a secret from you, while carrying on with their work lives just the same. You'll also find out what students do to drive teachers up the wall, and exactly how teachers feel when teenagers do and say certain things. You'll learn that, although professionals, teachers are also fallible, and, when pushed to the limit, they can "go off."

In chapters three through ten, you'll learn how to deal with each of the following problem teachers: the boor, the workaholic-martinet, the sarcastic insulter, the eyesore-earsore-nosesore, the soap opera star (the teacher who spends the entire period talking about personal things), the unfair teacher, the teacher who is chaotic, confused and out of control, and the "burnout."

In chapter eleven, you'll read about the wonderful teacher, and you'll find out how to bring out the "wonderful" in all of your teachers, especially the problem teachers. In chapter twelve, you'll discover who is responsible for your education and for your life—and why.

–I WOULDN'T TAKE THE JOB FOR A MILLION DOLLARS!!!–

Who in their right mind would want to become a teacher? I asked a variety of people from many walks of life the following question, just to see what they would say: "Since, as a nation, we will soon be facing the greatest teacher shortage in the history of America, would you be willing to consider a change in career and become a high school or junior high school teacher if the price were right?" Here are some of the answers I got.

Are you kidding. Not for a million dollars. I can't see how anybody would want to take on that job—especially in this day and age.

28-year-old lawyer

Not on your life. I can't even cope with two teenagers of my own. Try to tame thirty-some-odd teens and, at the same time, teach them anything when all they want to do is watch TV, think about drugs and sex, and cut class? No. Thank you very much. I'll pass.

44-year-old real estate broker

Money? Even if they gave me a starting salary of $150,000 a year, I would turn it down. It wouldn't be worth the drain on my energy and the frustration— and from what I read in the papers, the danger.

50-year-old store owner

–WHY DO PEOPLE BECOME TEACHERS?–

Not too long ago, someone coined a saying meant to put teachers down.

Those who *can*, do. Those who can't, teach.

I believe the opposite is true. In fact, it is those who *can* that teach, and what's more, it's those who are *"called"* that do. But more than that, it's those who are tough enough, and determined enough, and dedicated enough who stay in the profession.

Why do people become teachers? Is it the pay? It couldn't be that, because a lot more money could be made in the business world, even at a low-level job. Is it the summer vacations? I doubt it, especially since many teachers have to work in the summer to supplement their modest incomes in order to keep up with the rising cost of living. Is it laziness? That's highly unlikely, since it takes more energy to teach than to do jobs with twice the pay and half the problems. Is it job security? I doubt it, since, as you will see, teachers are regularly evaluated, "written up," laid off, and even fired. Is it lack of ambition? Not likely, since many teachers have left teaching and gone into other fields, quite successfully, only to return to teaching because they "missed the students."

So what is it that makes a person want to become a teacher? Teachers from all over the country tell me:

Teaching is a calling. A teacher can make "all the difference" in a young life. We can guide teens in the right direction—yes, even math teachers can do that.
Math teacher, 14 years

I wanted to do something worthwhile with my life. Teaching is more than a job. You can't put a price on the satisfaction you get from being able to influence a young life in a positive way.
American history teacher, 21 years

I've wanted to teach as far back as I can remember. I've always had the gift of being able to talk—to explain and to inspire.
Language arts teacher, 12 years

I like working with teens. They're not as set in their ways as adults. You can exert an influence.

French teacher, 15 years

I had my own business, but I sold it and became a teacher when I said to myself, "It's about time you started giving back."

Accounting teacher, 11 years

I had to choose between becoming a lawyer or a teacher. In the end, I chose teaching because it was more meaningful. I thought it would be better to spend my time showing people how not to get in trouble in the first place, rather than spend it trying to help them get out of trouble after the damage was done.

English teacher, 16 years.

The message is clear. Most people choose teaching as a career because they want to help people. Rather than spend their lives merely making money or feeding their own egos, they choose a profession where they can, as one teacher expresses it, "make all the difference."

True, there are some teachers who do not fit into this category. Most people who enter the profession for less than noble motives, however, either become "hooked" on helping people or get out fast. Here's why:

I became a teacher so I could get the summers off. But when I saw how much aggravation I had to put up with, I realized it wasn't worth it just for the summers. I was going to quit, but just then I started to like it. I began to enjoy the relationship I had with the students, and their appreciation when I went all out for them. If it were just for the summers off, I would have quit a long time ago.

Science teacher, 9 years

I didn't want to go to Viet Nam, so I became a teacher. But guess what? I ended up getting drafted anyway, and when I came back, I missed the kids, so I started teaching again. I'm still here.

Phys ed teacher, 12 years

There's something about teaching that's intoxicating. You begin to see how a little effort on your part can do so much to influence the entire course of so many young lives. Sometimes even in spite of yourself, you begin to pour your heart out trying to make a difference. So even if teaching were not much more than a "job" when you started, it quickly becomes a driving call—a mission. You find yourself forgetting the aggravation, the low pay, and the lack of respect you often receive from the "outside world." That's how obsessed you become with your chance to make a major difference in the future of the world by influencing the minds of your students.

–HOW DO YOU EXPLAIN THE MEANIES, THE BOORS, THE EYESORES AND THE BURNOUTS?–

But if this is so, what about all the teachers who seem not to care about the students—the rigid martinet (the disciplinarian who goes by the book, refusing to bend the rules), the dreadful boor who lulls you to sleep by his monotone voice, and the "burnout" who apparently stumbles out of bed in the morning and drags himself through the day, half alive, and so on?

The truth is, if you dig deep enough, even the meanest or most bored-looking teacher, deep down inside, has a flame still burning—the original fire that called him or her to the profession in the first place. The problem is, that flame has dwindled because of lack of fanning or "inspiration." But you can help to rekindle that flame. Yes. It is you, the student, who can inspire your teacher by giving just one minute of your time—but more of that later.

-THE GUARANTEE-

This book comes with my personal guarantee. If you read it from cover to cover and try out the ideas contained in it, you will improve your relationship with the teacher that is driving you crazy, and this improvement will translate into a better grade in that course. Instead of failing the course, you will not only pass it, but pass it with a higher mark than you could have gotten had you not read this book.

-IMPORTANT: DON'T SKIP CHAPTERS TWO AND ELEVEN-

When you look at the table of contents, you may become so excited about a given chapter (because you think you've spotted *your* teacher), that you will go right to it. You can do so if you please. However, no matter what you do, don't forget to go back and read chapter two, because it will give you insight into all teachers by telling you what goes on "behind the scenes" in both school and in their personal lives. In a way, you can think of me as an infiltrator. I am a teacher, you know, and for the first time in book publishing history, I'm giving away our secrets to teenagers.

Let me also ask you not to skip chapter eleven. It wouldn't be fair to have you read about boors, burnouts, martinets, and eyesores and never read about the majority of teachers—the wonderful ones.

-THERE'S NO SUCH THING AS A TOTAL ANYTHING-

And speaking of teachers labeled as boors, burnouts, martinets, and eyesores, let me make one thing very clear. There's no such thing as a *total* boor, a *total* burnout, or a *total* anything for that matter. I made these titles up for the sake of convenience—to highlight the way some teachers appear to certain students, so that the students can quickly identify their particular "problem" teachers.

Keep in mind that most teachers are not one "type" but a combination of "types," and then some. For example, your "unfair" teacher may also be brilliant, the "eyesore" may be very kind and funny, and so on. Even your wonderful teacher is probably not always all wonderful, but at times perhaps sarcastic, or even a soap opera star. You'll see what I mean later.

In the meantime, have fun. Everything written in this book has come from the mouth of either a teacher or a teenager. None of it has been made up. The names have been changed to protect the innocent (and the guilty!), on both sides of the desk.

-REMINDERS-

1. The goal of this book is to help you to pass your course with the highest grade possible, no matter how bad you think the teacher is.

2. You can skip around in this book if you want to, but don't neglect to read chapter two. It tells you a lot of secrets about what goes on behind the scenes in the lives of your teachers.

3. Most people wouldn't take on the job of teaching for a million dollars.

4. Teachers are underpaid and overworked. They became teachers and remain teachers because they love helping people and believe that they can be a positive influence on the younger generation.

5. Teachers are less than perfect for a lot of reasons. Chapters two through ten will explain why.

6. Chapter eleven describes the majority of teachers. Don't forget to read it.

7. This book comes with a guarantee: You will pass the course of your "problem teacher" with a higher mark if you read this entire book and apply the ideas in it. If you don't get these results, write to me immediately!!

2

Behind the Scenes: What Teachers Go Through!!!

A teacher's life is not easy. You only see your teacher for about forty minutes a day, and that's the end of it. Perhaps you never gave much thought to what happens to that person during the rest of the day.

Teachers have a lot more going on in their lives besides teaching and marking tests. This chapter will give you insight into what really goes on in their world. By the time you finish reading it, you may have a better understanding of why your teacher sometimes seems grouchy, sad, or tired.

We'll talk about everything from clerical chores to hall patrols. We'll discuss pressure from the teachers' bosses and peers. We'll also look at their personal problems and tragedies, and last but not least, we'll find out what annoys them most about certain students.

–CLERICAL CHORES AND OTHER NON-TEACHING "JOBS" THAT DRAIN TEACHERS' ENERGY–

Teachers are faced with numerous clerical and non-teaching jobs. If any of these many chores are not attended to on time, reminders and reprimands are sent. If the chore is still not done, the administration writes a letter reporting the incident, and it is placed in the teacher's "file" (a permanent record of the teacher's performance in that school).

Such letters are a real threat to teachers. Because most teachers are ultra-responsible, and also because they themselves regularly evaluate and write up reports on other people (students), they are highly sensitive to being "written up." So, no matter how unfair or time-consuming the chores may be, most teachers will try to accomplish them. But the extra jobs add stress to their daily lives.

In order to give you a general idea of what these chores are and how teachers feel about them, I asked teachers to tell me which non-teaching tasks they hate the most and why. Not surprisingly, every teacher had something to report:

> We're forced to do "building assignments" every other term during what would otherwise be our free period. This involves either patrolling the halls, guarding the door, working in the dean's office, or assisting in the lunchroom. How do they expect me to return to my class and be composed enough to teach a creative lesson when I've just come from a lunchroom of screaming teenagers who had a "food

fight,'' or just got cursed out by a student who refused to show me his hall pass? I went to college to be a teacher, not a security guard.

I hate the ''bubble sheets'' we have to fill out to report cutting. I teach 175 students a day, and for each of them, I must check class attendance against homeroom attendance. If they're cutting, I must ''bubble in'' the day. If I don't hand the sheets into my chairman at the end of the week, I get a letter of complaint. That's just one of a thousand clerical chores I have to do.

I don't know how it is in other school systems, but in New York City, someone came up with the brilliant rule that if a teacher is absent, and the school is unable to hire a substitute teacher, we must give up our lunch hour or preparation period and cover that class. We are paid the minimum substitute wage for that duty (you collect it three months later, and after taxes, you can hardly notice the difference in your pay). But the real issue is inconvenience. It doesn't matter that I may have made an important lunch meeting that day. It is no concern to them that I may have planned to mark tests on my prep period—tests that my students are anxiously waiting to have returned to them!! Why didn't I take that into consideration and plan ahead? Impossible. You get no notice whatsoever. You come into the building and discover a note on your time card. And woe be unto you if you should fail to see the note and somehow miss the assignment. Your name is called over the loudspeaker, and if you happen to be out of the building, you are severely rebuked and possibly ''written up.'' I can cope very well with my regular teaching duties, but extra burdens such as this can prove to be the proverbial "straw" that breaks the camel's back, which translates, in my case to "drive me out of teaching."

Every term we have to do what is called "break-up of permanent records." We have to pluck out the files of students according to their new homeroom and place them in their new homeroom record tray. This job takes at least three hours, and in June we do it in ninety-degree heat, with no air-conditioning. When I ask why teachers have to do this rather than a hired secretarial staff, the answer is always the same: It costs too much money. There's no room in the budget.

Those meaningless census reports are a bother to me. You have to count the number of students of various races, divide them by sex, and then justify the total with your register. Is this why I went to college for eight years—and studied English literature?

Adding up the numbers in the roll book at the end of the year is my nemesis. I'm not an accountant, and have never been good with figures, so inevitably I make errors in calculation. I would gladly hire someone to do the task for me, but there's a law stating that only teachers can write in the roll book: it's a legal document. We even have to sign a notarized statement swearing that our records are accurate.

And that's only the tip of the iceberg. There are also monthly attendance tallies, lunch tickets, transportation passes, etc., to be dealt with. Although teachers did not enter the profession to become secretaries or security guards, whether they like it or not they find themselves filling those roles. Such duties are tedious and time-consuming.

Don't forget that in addition to their non-teaching duties, teachers have a lot of after-school work related to teaching, such as marking homework and tests, placing marks on permanent records, preparing for the next day's classes, making calls and meeting with parents, attending regular staff and departmental meetings, supervising various extracurricular activities, and so on.

Now, add to this the pressure teachers get from their superiors, ranging from their immediate boss—the chairperson of their department, to their higher bosses—the assistant principal and the principal, and sometimes even the school board or school superintendent. They endure pressure from parents and from peers, from their unions and their bosses—and you.

–PRESSURE FROM THE DEPARTMENT CHAIRPERSON–

New teachers are observed by the chairperson often, until they have proven themselves. In most school systems, even veteran teachers are observed at least once a year, just to make sure that they're still teaching properly.

–THE PROCESS OF
BEING OBSERVED–

When observing a teacher, the chairperson sits in the back of the room and takes notes on how well the teacher conducts the lesson. The teacher is judged on his or her ability to capture the class's interest at the beginning of the lesson, to sustain class participation throughout the lesson, to teach the lesson with intellectual competence, and to stimulate curiosity for further learning.

In the New York City system, which in this respect is similar to many others, the chairperson writes up a detailed report after observing the teacher, who, in turn, reads and signs it. A copy is also placed in the teacher's file. If the report indicates any lack of competence, the teacher is given assistance and observed again. If the reports continue to indicate a problem, the teacher can eventually be fired.

Being observed always puts pressure on teachers, no matter how talented they are. Not only do they have to prepare an excellent lesson, but they have to depend upon student participation to make the lesson a success. For this reason, most teachers are a little nervous when being observed, and many don't discuss with their students what's going on.

Some teachers may just let the chairperson sit in the back of the room in the hope that the students will soon forget his or her presence. Other teachers may say to the class, "I bragged to the chairman about what a great class this is, so he wanted to come in and see for himself. Let's really give him a good show." This helps to take some of the pressure off the teacher, who is in fact being "tested."

–When A Chairperson
Makes Life Difficult
For Your Teacher–

Usually chairpersons are sympathetic toward teachers, whether they be new teachers or "old timers." But once in a while a chairperson may "have it in" for a certain teacher. When this happens, the chairperson will make frequent, unannounced visits to the classroom. Teachers who are under such pressure find themselves frequently watching the door for the dreaded "visit."

Even the greatest teacher in the world would probably not appreciate being continually watched, which creates a lot of stress. Looking back, can you remember a time when your teacher seemed upset while being observed?

Another source of pressure can be lesson plans. When a teacher is new, he or she is required to write up detailed daily lesson plans to be checked by the chairperson. After a while, however, teachers are usually allowed to teach from memory, the book, or whatever way feels comfortable. There are some chairpersons, however, who "go by the book" and demand that teachers show them lesson plans forever. This can be time-consuming and annoying. One teacher says:

> By now I don't need lesson plans. I know what I'm doing. Yet the new department chairman requires that I write up a plan every day. I've been teaching biology for the past twenty years and I know how to teach it. It's an annoying waste of time to ask me to write a plan each day. This chairman is making my life miserable. For the first time in my teaching career, I'm thinking of quitting.

–PRESSURE FROM THE PRINCIPAL–

The principal is the boss of the school. He or she has the power to rate a teacher as either satisfactory or unsatisfactory. If a teacher receives repeated unsatisfactory ratings, that teacher is in jeopardy of losing his or her job.

–HOW TEACHERS GET RATED UNSATISFACTORY–

Teachers do all sorts of things that can get them in trouble. I'm not talking about the extreme and unusual cases so diligently reported by the media in which teachers become sexually involved with students or get caught buying or using drugs. I'm referring to such "abuses" as letting a class out two minutes before the bell, allowing students to go to the lavatory without a pass, failing to turn in a lesson plan (even for a class they've been teaching for twenty years), coming a few minutes late to class, missing "hall patrol," refusing to do last minute covering of other teachers' classes, and so on.

Why do teachers break school rules and get into trouble with the principal? Often for the same reasons you do, but generally with a lot more provocation. Teachers are likely to feel that some of the school rules are too rigid or imposing, so they take it upon themselves to alter them. Since most schools are run rather strictly, teachers are usually severely rebuked for breaking any rules, even extremely minor ones. Even the most proficient teachers run a high risk of eventually getting fired if they continually break school rules, whether or not the breaking of those rules actually harms anyone. Because of this pressure to follow the rules, no matter how rigid and unreasonable they may seem, teachers experience a lot of stress—and may in turn seem rigid and unreasonable to you. After all, if they're going to be reprimanded for letting classes out two minutes early, even during the last day before the holidays, why should they give in to your demands to do so?

–THE TEACHER'S REPORT CARD–

At the end of each school year, teachers are rated by their principals on their performance in a number of different categories, as you can see from the New York City teacher rating sheet I've provided. Teachers are marked either "satisfactory" or "unsatisfactory" in each category. Just for fun, why don't you xerox this sheet and rate each of your teachers. Also, imagine what your teacher would get in each category if your principal were evaluating him or her. (The sheets differ in their details, of course, depending upon the school system, but New York's is typical of what teachers face at evaluation time.

A. Personal and Professional Qualities
  1. Attendance and punctuality
  2. Personal appearance
  3. Voice, speech, and use of English
  4. Professional attitude and professional growth
  5. Resourcefulness and initiative
B. Pupil Guidance and Instruction
  1. Effect on character and personality growth of pupils
  2. Control of class
  3. Maintenance of wholesome classroom atmosphere
  4. Planning and preparation of work

5. Skill in adapting instruction to individual needs and capacities
6. Effective use of appropriate methods and techniques
7. Skill in making class lessons interesting to pupils
8. Extent of pupil participation in classroom
9. Evidence of pupil growth in knowledge, skills, appreciation, and attitudes
10. Attention to pupil health, safety and general welfare

C. Classroom or Shop Management
1. Attention to physical conditions
2. Housekeeping and appearance of room
3. Care of equipment by teacher and children
4. Attention to records and reports
5. Attention to routine matters

D. Participation in School and Community Affairs
1. Maintenance of good relations with teachers and with supervisors
2. Effort to establish and maintain good relationships with parents
3. Willingness to accept special assignments in connection with school program

E. Additional Remarks

As you can see, there are categories for just about everything, so there are a couple of dozen ways of being rated unsatisfactory—more than enough to cause trouble for any teacher who for any reason is not liked by those in authority. This includes both the chairperson *and* the principal, even though only the latter performs the evaluation. Because the principal cannot effectively be aware of every teacher's performance in every category, he or she depends upon the department chairperson for much of the information that goes on the rating sheet.

You may have noticed that the principal occasionally walks into one of the classrooms in your school—probably in order to do a spot check and make sure that everything is in order. If the principal has a complaint about a teacher's class, a note will be placed in the teacher's mailbox requesting a meeting. When such a note is received, most teachers experience great stress (have a heart-attack), as you can imagine. Even the best teachers worry and wonder about what they might have done wrong.

Principals call teachers into meetings for a variety of offenses, not just classroom management. The charge could be leaving the building during a non-lunch period, not clocking in on time, or not showing up for hall patrol, lunchroom duty, or door guarding. If the offense continues, the teacher may receive an unsatisfactory rating.

The job of a principal is not easy. Often principals are just following rules made by *their* bosses, people who may not have seen the inside of a classroom for years and have little idea about how to run a school. But because the principals are the enforcers of these sometimes stupid rules, some teachers give the principal as hard a time as the most rebellious students give their teachers. In fact, it has been said that if you teach long enough, you eventually begin to behave like a recalcitrant student. It's the nature of the job, some people say. You can't fight them, so you join them.

–PEER PRESSURE–

–When Teachers "Report" Each Other–

When teachers sink to behaving like children, they can get very petty and even vindictive, not just with their students, but with their peers as well. Sometimes teachers will actually report each other to the principal for various misdemeanors. Teachers tell the principal: "Mrs. Jones never shows up at the staff meetings. Why is she allowed to get away with it and not I?" or "I saw Mr. Williams tear up his cutting sheets. Shouldn't he be forced to fill them out just like everybody else?" Teachers will report each other for everything from leaving the building early to sitting behind the desk instead of walking around the room. It's up to the discretion of the principal to decide what to do about such reports.

–TEACHERS REBEL AGAINST THE "CLOCK"–

Sometimes when teachers are not treated as professionals they behave in an unprofessional manner. Until recently, New York City teachers were required to clock in and out every day. In some schools, if a teacher punched in late, even by one minute, the time was added up, and at the end of the month, that teacher's check was "docked" for the amount of late time. The fact that most teachers leave school, only to put in several more hours of work at home, grading papers and preparing lessons, was of no interest to the makers of the time-clock policy.

At the end of the day, teachers were not allowed to punch out even one minute before the official clock-out time. If they did, the time was circled on the card, and the teacher was sent a warning letter. If the behavior was not stopped, eventually the teacher was "written up." So at the end of the day, in most schools, one could observe long lines of teachers with card in hand, patiently waiting by the clock until "the time."

Mysteriously, some things would sometimes happen to these time clocks. Paper clips would be found in them, silly putty painted over them, crazy glue poured into them, and worse. In fact, in one New York City high school, during a Christmas party when the students were out of the building and the teachers and staff were preoccupied, someone poured liquid metal into the time clock, smeared tar all over it, and then plastered time cards onto the tar. The clock was rendered useless. Needless to say, it was only a matter of time before a new clock was installed.

The late Chancellor Green demanded the end of the time clock, calling it an unnecessary burden upon teachers. But unfortunately, it has been replaced by an equally asinine system. Teachers are now required to move their cards from one side of the rack to the other upon arrival and departure. Teachers who neglect to do this are punished by being required to punch in and out. Anyone who refuses to punch in and out is "written up" and is eventually given disciplinary action.

In other words, teachers are kept on a short leash and are expected to follow orders unquestioningly. If they don't, their jobs are threatened. Though the examples I give are from my own school system, problems that are equally petty and equally irritating plague teachers in most systems. Teachers resent such treatment, since they are professionals and have gone to school for years to become experts in their subject areas. Given their dedication and training, they would like the same autonomy and respect that professionals in other areas, like medicine and law, take for granted. But unlike doctors and lawyers, they are often treated like naughty children who have to be monitored every minute for possible disobedience. Is it any wonder that they're sometimes resentful?

–PERSONAL PROBLEMS: YOU MAY NEVER KNOW IT BUT . . .–

In addition to the clerical work and pressures from the chairperson, the principal, and the teacher's own peers, there are other things that weigh upon the teacher—personal problems like those all human beings have. I know you know this, but I also know how easy it is to forget it. We've all had the experience in our student days of running into a teacher in a department store or a movie theater or a restaurant and being stunned. It's always amazing to realize that the teacher really *is* a human being, which is why we're so surprised by these perfectly normal encounters.

Teachers have arguments with their husbands, wives, and children just like everybody else. They take difficult and time-consuming courses after school. They have bills to pay and not enough money to pay them. People in their families get sick and die. Yet in spite of it all, most teachers continue teaching, and most of them never let their students know that they are going through a hard time. Teachers say:

> My father died a slow death of cancer. I continued to teach, because in the classroom I could escape my sadness for a few hours each day. Some of my more perceptive students would notice my sadness and ask me what was wrong, but I didn't want to burden them with my problems. I figured they had teenage troubles of their own and didn't need to hear mine.

> I have five children. My wife left me, and I had to take care of them by myself. I never told my students

any of it, but I felt as if I were walking around in a daze most of the time. Now things are back to normal because I've remarried. But that was a rough time for me.

I had a miscarriage. The students never even knew that I was pregnant in the first place, so they had no idea why I was feeling so miserable. I kept it to myself and tried to get through each day—but it wasn't easy. At times I snapped at them at the slightest provocation. I guess they thought I was just being moody.

My brother became a drug addict and was committed to a rehabilitation center. He dominated my mind, and I found myself unable to teach with my usual energy and enthusiasm. It's really difficult to face a class full of teenagers every day when something is eating away at you.

My teenage daughter and I are not getting along. It's hard to keep your mind on teaching when you've just had an hour-long screaming match with a child who is threatening to run away from home.

Last night my boyfriend broke up with me. Did I feel like coming to work and dealing with my students today?

My son was caught stealing. Now he's on probation and they suggest I put him in therapy. I'm really upset about it.

Chances are, your teacher is not going through an emotional crisis, but a more mundane one. Even day to day problems can cause a teacher to become anxious or distraught.

My car has broken down five times this month. Without a car, I have to get up an hour earlier to take public transportation to work. I also get home an hour later. Yet I have to remain the same cheerful person with the students, or I'm a dead man.

I got home from work and the roof of my house had caved in. On top of that, the heating system was destroyed because the cold had burst the pipes.

And on and on and on. So, if your teacher is slightly preoccupied, a little under the weather, oddly unpleasant, or "moody," stop and think: "He may be having some problems right now." Instead of making his life more difficult, why not try to be helpful? You can cheer your teacher up with a friendly smile and a pleasant "Good morning." You could even say something kind to your teacher—something that shows that you're sympathetic even though you don't know what he's going through.

–WHEN TEENAGERS GIVE TEACHERS A HARD TIME–

In addition to all of the above pressures, certain things that teenagers say and do add to a teacher's daily stress. I asked teachers to give me examples of student behavior that really "gets to them." They had plenty to say.

It really bothers me when students ask for the pass and then abuse it by hanging out in the hall for half the period. Then when you refuse them the pass the next time, they "cop an attitude."

It's a drain on my energy when a teenager acts like a baby. One student wanted me to do the equivalent of change her diaper every day. She would never bring her own computer disk, but instead ask for mine. Then she would ask questions I had answered a hundred times before. She behaved as if she thought she was the only student in my class.

Incessant jabbering. There was one boy in my class who would never stop talking. No matter what I did, he just kept yapping away. It got to the point where I had him physically removed by the guard.

Inconsiderate students really bug me. One girl would come late every day, knocking into things as she made her way to her seat, all the time talking loudly. When she sat down, she would make sure she banged her books hard against the desk.

Gum chewing bothers me. Why? I have to stand in front of the class and look at a herd of cows chewing at the cud. It's not a pretty sight to see. In fact, it's downright disgusting after a while.

I can't stand the sound of snapping gum. But what bothers me even more than the gum snapping is when after you've just seen them with the gum, they deny it and open their mouths so wide you can see way down to their tonsils.

Zombyism. This boy would sit in the back of the room and act like a mummy. No matter what I said to him, he would not respond, not answer me. I felt like whacking him in the head.

Hello! Is anybody out there? When I'm trying like a madman to make a point, it is most disheartening to hear a series of yawns.

When a teacher is in front of the room pouring his or her heart out to the students, and the teens behave as if they could care less, a teacher is not only frustrated and angry, he or she is disgusted. "I'm wasting my life," he thinks. "I'm fighting an impossible battle," she says.

Most teachers are natural "hams." They love an audience and are looking for some feedback. If you sit there nonchalantly snapping your gum or staring into space, you can bet that your teacher will become annoyed and even indignant. Your teacher is giving her all to make what she believes to be an important point, and there you sit, acting as if you're about to fall asleep.

Put yourself in the teacher's place. How would you feel if you were in front of a group, talking about something you really believed in, and no one appeared to be paying attention?

If you were the teacher, which student would you appreciate—the student who appeared interested, who took the time to ask a question and to make eye contact, or the one who seemed to ignore you? Which student do you think would be more likely to get a good grade?

Do you realize how simple it would be for you to get along better with your teacher? All you have to do is show a little respect. If the teacher doesn't like gum chewing, don't chew. When the teacher is talking, be quiet. Look directly at him and nod your head, indicating that you're getting the point. Be considerate of the teacher. If you go out of the room on a pass, return quickly and don't make a disturbance in getting back to your seat.

I know what you're saying right now. That's no fun!! Right. But it will probably help to raise your grade quite a bit. In the following chapters, you will learn how to handle teachers of each particular personality type so that, no matter how bad the situation is, you can pass the course with the highest mark possible. You don't have to be a genius to put these ideas to work. All it will take is an adventurous spirit, the willingness to try something new—and maybe even some genuine sympathy for your teacher.

–REMINDERS–

1. Teachers have lots of clerical and other "chores" that must be completed during a school day. These obligations can sap the teacher's energy and steal the teacher's time.

2. Teachers endure pressure from their superiors. They can feel "under the gun" when they are threatened with unsatisfactory ratings and letters in their file.

3. Your grouchy or irritable teacher may be going through a personal crisis. Have a heart.

4. Teachers are natural "hams." They love an audience. The highest compliment you can pay your teacher is to listen with rapt attention when he or she is making a point.

5. If certain things annoy your teacher, why not stop doing those things? Let's face it. One way or another, your behavior will affect your grade.

6. You are in a position to make your teacher's life happier. When you do that, you make your own school life more pleasant and greatly increase your chances of getting a good grade.

7. In the following chapters you will find out how to handle even the most difficult teachers.

3

It's Booooring!!!!

"What a bore. I could fall asleep just listening to that teacher!!!" Did you ever feel that way? Of course you did. So what did you do in that class? Chances are you leaned back in your chair and daydreamed about what you were going to do after school, or thought about some other pleasant subject. If your seat was conveniently located in the back of the room, maybe you actually did fall asleep. The point is, you arranged a way for yourself to "escape" from the disagreeable situation.

When something is distasteful, the natural instinct is to try to get away from the source of offense. However, in the case of a boring course in school, since you have to pass that course in order to graduate, there is no escaping—merely delaying. You're stuck. But there *is* some good news. You can change the situation by taking control of what's happening in the class. You can make that class less boring. But how?

The suggestions I make in this chapter will at first seem like a game, but after a short period of time, you'll find yourself becoming so interested in the subject matter of the course that you'll forget you were playing a game in the first place. In fact, you'll begin to learn things you never even thought you cared about. What's more, you will begin to feel intelligent, because you will become knowledgeable about things you had never thought about before. In the end, you'll not only pass that dreaded "boring" class, but you'll probably get a much higher grade than you ever dreamed possible. *And* you'll feel good about yourself.

In this chapter, we'll discuss various types of boring situations: the boring subject, the teacher who makes you copy endless notes, the teacher with the monotone voice, the repetitious teacher, and so on. The goal will be to make that class more interesting, to learn the material required, and, of course, to get the highest mark possible.

–DO YOU HAVE TO FAIL A CLASS JUST BECAUSE IT'S BORING?–

I asked high school students to think of a class they failed because they were bored and to tell me if they think they *could have passed* the class if they really wanted to. They said:

I hate social studies and always have. The subject itself is so boring that even if the teacher was great, I would still think it was boring. I just think it's stupid to learn about the past. I have enough trouble dealing with the present and worrying about my future. Why should I jam up my brain with all kinds of "facts" that I have no use for? I could have passed if only I was interested in ancient history. But I'm not.

Donna, 14

I failed biology because the teacher was extremely boring. She must have thought she was writing a novel on the board—it was endless. Nothing I wrote and nothing she said ever travelled through my brain. Truthfully, I could have passed if I had forced myself to concentrate and pay attention.

Ricky, 15

All my math teacher did was repeat himself a hundred times. I used to cover my ears when he spoke. I started cutting the class, because just the thought of having to sit through one of those broken-record lectures would give me a headache. Then when I came to class I couldn't understand anything, because I had missed too much work. I know I would have passed if I had only kept coming to class. Now I have to go to summer school. My vacation is ruined.

Tricia, 16

Why do English teachers insist on giving us stupid books to read? Who wants to learn about some dumb animals who take over a farm? If it's supposed to be about Communism, why can't the man just talk about Communism in the first place and not waste all that time bringing in the animals—then we have to figure out what he's really talking about. I failed the class because I didn't finish that book, and when I tried to bluff my way, the teacher realized I didn't know what I was talking about. Looking back I realize that I could have at least passed with a 65 or 70.

Billy, 16

Each of these students has a legitimate complaint, but nothing that couldn't have been worked out. As they admit, it was not the difficulty of the work that caused them to fail, but their inability to concentrate on something that bored them. Let's see what they could have done to pass their courses.

–WHEN YOU HAVE ABSOLUTELY NO INTEREST IN A SUBJECT—OR A TEACHER–

Donna resents learning about history. She can't see how it relates to her life, present or future, so she closes her mind to the subject and refuses to learn anything. If you feel this way about one of your classes, here's an idea.

A good way to get "into" a subject is to become curious about it. But how can you do that if you have no interest in it to begin with? It's simple. While the teacher is lecturing, no matter how boring the subject or the person who is teaching it, listen attentively *with the goal of thinking up a question to ask about what she's saying.* Once you get one in your mind, force yourself to raise your hand and ask it.

Make it a goal to ask one question each class period for the first week. Then ask two per class period the second week, and finally three per class period the third week. Then continue to ask at least three questions per class period until the end of the semester. What will happen if you do this? You'll not only pass the course, but you'll also get a much higher mark than you would have gotten had you tuned the teacher out and not participated in the class. Why?

First of all, you will have retained more material. In order to ask questions, you have to listen to the lecture instead of just daydreaming. If you actively listen, the information travels through your brain and is registered there. Otherwise, it never makes the trip, as Ricky said.

Once you start asking questions, no matter how forced they are at first, you will eventually find yourself asking about things you are genuinely curious about. As new light is shed on various aspects of the subject, you will become more and more interested in that subject and, to your surprise, will discover that you are actually retaining information about it—sometimes without even trying.

Third, you will soon become hooked on thinking. You will begin to challenge some of the statements your teacher makes and will ask for explanations. You'll begin feeling smart—and you may like that feeling.

Fourth, the teacher will begin to respect you. She will see you in a new light. Your curiosity and interest will inspire her and make *her* teaching day less boring—which may in fact make her teaching less boring too. Everybody needs a little feedback and reinforcement. She may even begin to look your way when making certain points, in expectation of your response.

Fifth, your teacher will be more likely to give you special help if you need it and would probably be willing to spend some of her free time working with you.

With all of this, when mark time comes around, what do you think will happen?

–HOW TO DEAL WITH A TEACHER WHO "BOARD WORKS" YOU TO DEATH–

Ricky complains about too much board work (tedious copying). He resents having to write and write and write, claiming that nothing he copies actually registers in his brain. What could he do to change the situation?

Whenever you're forced to take lots of class notes, you have a golden opportunity to organize them in a personalized way. Ricky could highlight his notes, using a system like the one I'm about to suggest or one of his own devising. For example, he could use yellow highlighter for things in the notes that he already fully understands, red for things he needs to concentrate on a little more, blue for things that need even more work, and green for those things that he doesn't understand at all. Then for each "green" section, he could write up a question to ask the teacher.

Don't worry about asking a question that might expose your "ignorance." Teachers are starving for interested students, are always happy when students ask questions, and are especially impressed when a student takes the time to write questions down as the result of class note-taking. It indicates to the teacher that this student takes the subject seriously.

If you put into practice all of the above, it's inevitable that your mark will go up—for all of the same reasons mentioned before: You will retain more of the subject matter, you will develop an interest in it, you will participate more in class, and you will develop a positive relationship with your teacher.

–WHAT IF MY FRIENDS LAUGH AT ME WHEN I CONTINUALLY ASK QUESTIONS IN CLASS?–

"But I can't raise my hand and ask questions. I'd be too embarrassed," you say. Nonsense. Forget about your classmates. Are they going to take the SAT's and the achievement tests for you? Are they going to give you a job when you graduate? Are they going to pay your rent? Of course not. So you'd better think about yourself, and survive.

Anyway, your classmates will not laugh for long. At

first they'll be surprised when you start asking questions and probably giggle a little, but in time they'll actually enjoy listening to you and begin to wonder what you'll ask next. In fact, you'll be doing them a favor because by amusing them, you'll be helping to keep them awake. Some of them might even start participating in class, too. Before you know it, everyone will be asking questions, and the class will be interesting enough to make you wonder where the time went when the bell rings. Everyone will be happy. When you come to think of it, the students in the class have a lot more power than they realize—power to determine the way each class session goes. Since you have to be there anyway, you might as well enjoy it as much as you can.

–LOOK AT THE BIG PICTURE—PUT OFF IMMEDIATE GRATIFICATION–

Now let's talk about Tricia's problem. She couldn't stand the repetitious math teacher so she covered her ears and eventually started cutting. This is always a mistake, and in math it's a disaster because if you don't learn step one, it's a good bet you won't understand step two, and so on. Before you know it, you're lost.

Had Tricia "bitten the bullet" and disciplined herself to listen to the repetitious teacher instead of taking the easy way out and cutting class, she would have heard what was being taught, learned the concepts, and passed the course, and not had to go to summer school. Tricia's problem is shortsightedness and lack of self-control. She ran away without first stopping to consider the price of her truancy. Giving in to her need to escape from an unpleasant situation, she simply created another one for herself. It is only after it's too late that she considers the inevitable consequences. Then she wishes that she had forced herself to attend class.

You can endure a repetitious teacher, and you know it. Would it kill you to sit there and endure hearing things said twice? Of course not. You could certainly learn the subject if you forced yourself to pay attention and to ask questions.

You can learn from your mistakes and the mistakes of others. Think ahead. The next time you're in a troublesome situation and are about to react in a hasty manner, stop and think before you act. Project the consequences of your behavior.

For example, if you're tempted to cut a class, think of how you'll feel next semester when you have to attend evening school, or worse, in the hot summer, when you have to repeat the course. Then think of how you'll feel if you tough it out now and pass the course.

The same rule applies for those who don't actually fail classes but get much lower marks than they could have gotten had they put more into the course. Think about your own experience. Did you ever settle for a mark that was ten or twenty points less than you could have gotten just because the subject was "boring" and you didn't want to put in any more time than the bare minimum? Don't you now wish you had paid the price and given it more effort?

–YOU LEARN MORE IN MATH THAN MATH–

The bonus in doing this is the carryover or the training effect. Each time you discipline yourself not to take the easy way out but to think of the consequences and do what is required to achieve your goal, you build inner strength. Once you see what your self-discipline has netted you—passed courses, higher grades, increased learning and parental approval—your self-esteem rises. You say to yourself, "I can overcome obstacles. I can effect changes in my life. I'm in control." And instead of developing the habit of running away from petty annoyances or even difficult challenges, you develop the habit of facing them head on, and conquering them.

So many people miss the point about school. It's not always the content of a particular course that's important; it's really the way you handle the challenge. To take the example of the math course, you may never use that math in your life for anything but passing the test with the best grade you can, but you will use the discipline and self-control it took to get through the course. And what you will have gained in self-esteem and self-control will serve you for the rest of your life.

–WHY DO WE HAVE TO READ THIS STUPID BOOK?–

If English teachers were asked to pick out the most common complaint they hear, it would probably be: "Why do we have to read this stupid book?" It seems obvious that if given a choice, teenagers would never select the same book as the teacher. Why?

If you were to choose a book, you would more than likely select a subject that you already know something about or are already interested in: love and romance, sex, cars, sports, horror—etc. This is all well and good, and in fact, you should pursue subjects of your own interest in your free time. However, it is the job of your school to offer you an opportunity to expand your horizons. In fact, that's the very purpose of education—to develop and enhance your knowledge. In order to do this, your teachers must ask you to read books you would not consider reading on your own. It is the teacher, the "expert," who is paid to lead your mind in a direction that it would not ordinarily take.

If the teacher were going to let everyone choose whatever he or she wanted to read, she wouldn't need to teach anything, would she? People read books that interest them all the time, and they don't take courses to read them. It's the books you don't choose to read on your own that require our assistance.

No one is saying you have to like the required book, or become thrilled and excited after reading each page, although it has been known to happen. As long as you read it, you've done your part. Then, if you wish, you can give an intelligent criticism of the book on your report or exam, explaining what you didn't like about it. In fact, teachers appreciate well-thought-out criticism. What they don't appreciate is a comment such as, "This book is dumb," from a student who has used his dislike for the book as an excuse not to read it.

Had Billy read *Animal Farm* instead of just complaining about how stupid the book was, he could have later expressed all of his objections on the test or book report. For example, he could have said that using the metaphor of animals in the barnyard to say something about communism was not very effective. So long as he demonstrates an awareness of what the author was trying to do, he's certainly entitled to his own opinion as to whether it was done well. He could also have argued that *Animal Farm*, in his opinion, is political satire, not literature, and should, therefore, be read in a history course rather than an English course. By demonstrating knowledge of the book, and only then expressing a critical opinion, he would have insured himself of more than a passing mark, even if he disagreed with the teacher about the value of the book.

When confronted with a book you don't want to read, the first thing to do is face the fact: You will have to read this book in order to pass the course. So, rather than waste your energy arguing with the teacher or brooding over the unfairness of the world, begin the job and start reading. Sometimes you'll surprise yourself and end up liking a book you dreaded having to read. My seventeen-year-old daughter recently experienced this very thing. She was assigned the Thomas Hardy novel, *Tess of the D'Urbervilles*. As stated by her, "I didn't want to read it because in the beginning, it seemed like a dreary book by an ancient author." After getting past the first chapter, she couldn't put it down. In fact, she ended up loving the book. "It was all about love and romance, and broken hearts. I could really relate to the main character. I felt for her. I enjoyed reading about someone's emotional pain. It gave me insight I didn't have before."

Most high schools have a "curriculum" for each grade level that requires that a given list of books be read. So chances are your English teacher has assigned a book she must teach you, whether she likes it or not (much less whether you like it or not). Other times, teachers are given autonomy, and allowed to assign books that they happen to love even if they're not on the list, as long as the chairperson approves. But if this is the case—if the teacher loves the book and has chosen it herself—don't even dream that you will be able to convince her that it's "stupid" and that she should pick a book that you like. Why would she listen to someone who hasn't read it when she has?

-LIFE IS NOT
A TELEVISION SHOW-

To say, "this is boring" and then not read the assigned book is to say, "I believe the world should entertain me. Life is a big television and if I don't like what's happening, I'll just use the remote control." The fact is, however, in the real world, we can't just "tune out" anything that is not thrilling, or that we find too challenging.

Life is not all fun and entertainment. In fact, life consists of a lot of goal-oriented work that is often tedious and difficult and requires self-discipline and self-control to accomplish.

You probably have more experience in goal-oriented activity than you think. Didn't you read the boring driver's manual in order to pass the road test, or bring your grades up to qualify for a school team, or do that humdrum clerical work last summer to buy the stereo system you wanted? People sometimes put up with a lot in order to reach their goals. They memorize all sorts of facts for job advancement or a higher salary, they read complicated instruction booklets in order to find out how to operate certain machinery, and on and on. So when a teacher assigns a book to read, just think of it as good training for life and get on with the job.

–WHAT TEACHERS SAY WHEN STUDENTS COMPLAIN, "THIS IS BORING"!!!–

Teachers become highly indignant when students complain that the work is boring. They tell me that their response to the student is usually something like:

This is not boring. You're boring, because you have no interest in anything.

English teacher, 4 years

I'm not here to entertain you.

Physics teacher, 11 years

If you paid attention and did the work, it wouldn't be boring.

English teacher, 21 years

Boring is in the eyes of the beholder. Interesting people never get bored.

Fashion design teacher, 6 years

Too bad. You have to do it anyway.

Science teacher, 7 years

Boring? Good. Then I know I'm doing my job.

Calculus teacher, 17 years

Maybe I should dance around with a pointed hat and ring bells while I teach. Would that excite you?

Math teacher, 27 years.

So, boring or not, instead of wasting time complaining about your work, why not use the techniques discussed in this chapter? They're guaranteed to make the subject less boring, which will help you not only to pass the course, but to get the highest grade possible.

–REMINDERS–

1. You never have to fail a class just because it's "boring." You can pass it, often at a level ten to twenty points higher than you ever dreamed possible.

2. You can keep yourself interested in a subject by making it your business to ask from one to three questions per class period.

3. If you're tempted to cut a class because it's "boooring," realize that no one ever died from attending a boring class. On the other hand, some people do have to go to summer school because they failed a class—and you could be one of them.

4. When you use self-discipline, you build inner strength that will help you overcome obstacles through all the years to come. The end result is higher self-esteem and a more fulfilling life.

5. If your English teacher assigns a book you think is boring, instead of wasting energy complaining about it, read the book and channel your frustration into an intelligent criticism of the work.

6. Teachers are not favorably impressed with students who continually say, "This is boring." I'm one of those teachers, and here's my answer to those students: Life

is not a television show. In the real world, you can't "tune out" unpleasant chores. It is not a thrill to read the driver's manual, yet people do it to achieve a goal. Your goal is to pass your course with a decent grade.

4

The Martinet and the Workaholic

"Martinet—a very strict disciplinarian, or stickler for rigid regulations." Did you ever meet a martinet? I'll bet you did. Your notebook heading must be exactly the way Martinet wants it. If you come to the class five seconds late, Martinet demands a late pass. If you miss a test, you cannot make it up. Martinet will not even accept a doctor's note. You know the type—teachers who go by the book, who refuse to bend the rules, no matter what the circumstances.

The workaholic often shares the same characteristics as the martinet, only in addition, the workaholic piles on the work, demanding the impossible. Then, if you don't do the work, you fail the course.

The first time I called someone a martinet was when I was in high school myself. I had recently learned the word and was probably subconsciously waiting to find someone who fit the description.

One day, when in the lunchroom, I left my assigned table and went to sit with some friends at another table. This was against the rules. No sooner did I sit down, than a mean-looking male teacher marched over to me with a bearing that was extremely rigid and military-like. He ordered me to go back to my table and I protested. The argument continued but no matter what I said, he refused to bend the rules. Finally, in anger, I blurted out, "You're such a martinet," and I returned to my table. Following me, he said, "You're not getting away with that."

The next day, however, he came over to me and told me that he hadn't meant to appear so rigid and unbending, and added: "But if I don't follow the rules, I can get in trouble, and if I let you get away with it, everyone else might do it, too, and we'll have chaos here." At that point, I began to feel sorry for him. And from that day on, I understood something about the nature of the martinets among us. They're usually nice people who are scared. They've probably gotten into trouble in the past for breaking rules, or have lost control when the rules were broken, so they feel compelled to "go by the book." Any deviation from the rules can seem extremely threatening to them.

Once you learn to understand what makes a martinet so rigid, you can stop feeling angry and find ways to make your life with that person more bearable. In this chapter, we'll look at martinets and workaholics of various degrees, and we'll find ways to "work around" them so that you pass their courses with the highest marks possible. Remember: You will have the power to pass these courses no matter what. From now on, if you fail, it will be because you didn't think it was worth the effort to make some minor changes in your behavior. You'll see what I mean as you read the chapter.

The following teachers are difficult to "live with," even for forty to fifty minutes a day. But since not all of your teachers will be martinets, you can learn to tolerate the ones who are. We'll start with the teachers who are easiest to deal with and end with the most difficult.

–TAKE OUT THAT GUM–

My teacher gives zeros for chewing gum. She will even lower your final grade by five points if you continue to chew gum.

Lisa, 16

The teacher who demands that you not chew gum in class is the easiest to satisfy. All you have to do to get her off your back is not chew gum. (I should know—I'm one of them). The minute you leave her class you can put the gum back in your mouth. Now what's so hard about that? "But I like to chew gum," you say. "It relaxes me." Is it relaxing when the teacher yells at you and threatens to lower your grade? Is it relaxing to worry that you may get caught every time the teacher looks your way? Of course not. It's a lot more relaxing not to have to worry about the gum at all, and so easy, too.

If it's so easy, then what's the problem? Why do you hate to refrain from gum chewing in a class when a teacher asks you to? The gum chewing is not really the issue; it's a matter of giving in. You don't want the teacher to win, so you try to outsmart her. "I'll do as I please," you think. "Why can't I chew gum if I feel like it?" But is playing that game worth it?

No, it isn't. Some teachers really will lower your grade just for gum chewing, because it annoys them, and because they see your refusal to cooperate as an act of defiance.

"Not fair," you say. "They're not supposed to lower grades for behavior." But what if they do it? What can you do? You can bring your mom or dad in, of course. Then what will happen? Your parent will have a conference with the teacher, and the teacher will agree to raise your grade back to where it should be if you agree to stop chewing gum. Chances are your parents will agree to this and in the end, you'll have to give up your gum anyway. Only now, you'll have your parent on your back in addition to your teacher, because parents have much better things to do with their time than get involved in silly disputes like that.

–I WANT IT DONE MY WAY–

I handed in my weekly homework to my global history teacher on my usual notebook paper, 5 by 7, but he refused to accept it because it wasn't on standard 8 by 10 paper. He made me copy ten pages of work over, just because he's an old fool.

Tamara, 14

My teacher won't accept the composition unless it's perfectly neat. You're not allowed to cross out. If you make a mistake, you must copy the entire thing over again.

Victor, 14

If the heading on every piece of paper is not exactly right, my teacher won't accept it. If a fire broke out in the school, I think that lady would be making kids fix their headings before they could leave her room.

Abby, 13

If the teacher demands that you do your work on a certain size paper, or in a certain style of notebook, or that the heading be done a certain way, or that your work be perfectly neat, resign yourself to the fact that she's not going to change her mind. You might as well get used to it and do it her way. Why call special attention to yourself over a minor issue? If you make yourself a target right from day one, your life in that class will be miserable. It's not worth it. Save your energy for bigger problems.

I don't say this because I'm a martinet myself. As far as I'm concerned, students can write their work on any size or color paper. In fact, one day, when a student complained that she didn't have any paper and couldn't do the work, I called her bluff and told her that she could write it on toilet paper. Wouldn't you know, she took me up on it. Then, as luck would have it, the principal came in when I was marking the work. When he saw the toilet paper, he just shook his head and walked out of the room. Lucky for me he has a sense of humor.

But most teachers are not like me, and most principals are not like him—some are totally the opposite, being "sticklers" for certain things. Who knows why? You might as well practice handling them, because in the real world, you will also meet such people (which is one reason many teachers give you for their demanding ways—to prepare you for what you'll encounter in the future). It just isn't worth your time and energy to do battle with them. And if you won, what would be your pitiful victory? The right to write on small non-standard size paper or cross things out? Wouldn't you rather save your energy for bigger battles? Don't use up all your ammunition for something so petty.

Sometimes we refuse to give a teacher satisfaction, even though it would be very easy to do. Why?—often out of a combination of plain old stubbornness and ego. Why should we give in? Why can't the other person give in? Well, in the case of a teacher, I can answer the question. You should give in because at this point in time, your teacher has power over your life. It's only a little power, I'll agree, but power nonetheless—the power to grade you, which can affect your future. So be smart and don't provoke your teacher unnecessarily.

Why do some teachers make a big deal of it if you

refuse to conform? For some, your refusal to follow the rules indicates a lack of respect for them. The simple act of refusing to write on the prescribed paper or to do the heading in a certain way may seem to them to be the equivalent of saying, "I don't respect your authority." Others do genuinely feel that they're preparing you for the standards you'll be expected to meet in more advanced schoolwork or on the job. Try arguing with your college teacher about the format of your term paper, or your boss about the way she wants a report written. You'll have even less luck with them than with the average high school teacher.

-JUST COME TO CLASS ON TIME-

If I come two minutes late, my Spanish teacher won't let me in. Then I have to waste another ten minutes getting a late pass.

Darin, 16

In a situation such as Darin's, where the teacher will not tolerate a student coming even one minute late without a pass, there's nothing you can do but come on time or get the pass. Why? Because technically, the teacher is right. If that teacher refuses to bend the rules by even a minute, it's better for you to comply than to get angry. What would that accomplish? You would only, as mentioned before, cause that teacher to focus on you. It would be much better for you to resign yourself to getting the late pass and put the whole episode behind you. If you're polite and reasonable, even when you don't think the teacher is, you may be able to change his attitude toward you and pave the way for a better relationship in the future.

Why won't the teacher let a student in a minute after the bell? Well, as discussed in the opening paragraphs of this chapter, a large part of the nature of the martinet is his fear of loss of control. He fears that if he lets one student in after the bell, all of the students may start coming late, so he has to "lay down the law" right from the start. This is the only way he can feel in control. He may also not want to face the consequences of allowing his students to break the rules. He may well have his own martinets to account to—his bosses or even his trouble-making, tale-bearing peers.

–IF YOUR TEACHER IS A SUPER-MARTINET–

My typing teacher won't even let me touch the typewriter keys. I mean, even if my hand is just resting on the keys, she accuses me of playing with them.

Sammy, 15

Mrs. Williams was worse than a drill master. Everything you said or did, you had to raise your hand—even to get up to throw something in the wastebasket. One day I got up and threw a paper in the basket without asking, and Dragon Lady (that's what we called her) made me take it out of the garbage.

Rythelle, 15

No matter what you do, this teacher will find something to yell about. Her voice could make a dog cry. Sit up straight, take off your hat, get a haircut, don't sniffle, speak up—she was worse than my mother. I hope she doesn't have any kids, for their sake.

Jerome, 15

Once you learn how to deal with moderate martinets, it's not so difficult to deal with the super-martinet. The principle is the same: All you have to do is give in to their little demands. I say "little," because, if you think about it, chances are that what they're asking you to do is more annoying than difficult.

Think of the above cases. How much effort would it take for Sammy to keep his hands entirely off the keys? Or for Jerome to cooperate with his teacher's demand for the 50 minutes a day he spends in her class—especially since most of those demands sound reasonable. And although I would agree with anyone who said that Rythelle's teacher is being ridiculous to make her take a piece of paper out of the basket just because she hadn't asked permission to throw it there in the first place, I still say that it will be easier for her in the long run if she makes a promise to herself to give in to the teacher on these minor points.

Although they're minor, these are the kinds of things that certain teachers will not compromise on, so there's no point in waging a war about them. If you win (and you almost never will), you'll have won the right to something so small that you may actually be embarrassed to have fought over something so petty, not to mention sorry to have won your teacher's enmity as a result. So don't allow yourself to be dragged down to such a petty level. You've got better things to do with your time, even if your teacher doesn't.

-THE IMPOSSIBLE
SITUATION-

Just because I left out my closing statement, my art teacher gave me a zero and insisted that I do the entire project over. The project took me two months to do. I could have rewritten the closing statement in about ten minutes. But just because she's so rigid and cruel, she demanded that I do an entirely new project from scratch.

Joanne, 16

In some cases the degree of injustice is so great that you just can't give in to the demands of your teacher. Joanne's case is one of them. Joanne should neither do the project over, nor quietly accept the zero. Instead she should report the situation to her parents and have one of them come in to see the department chairperson and the principal too, if necessary.

There's no reason why you, or any other student for that matter, should accept blatantly unfair treatment. Believe it or not, there are some very fair-minded people in most schools, and if you persist, with your parents' help you can usually obtain justice.

If this is true, one wonders why students don't bring parents in more often to plead their rightful causes. You know the answer to that better than I do. Many students fear that once a parent comes in, a teacher will report to their parents other things they have done wrong, such as cutting a class, missing homework assignments, being rude, and so on.

Don't fall victim to this trap, or allow guilt for past offenses to cloud your thinking. If you let your rights be taken away from you just because you fear being found out for former offenses, you'll regret it in the long run.

Even if your teacher did report past misdeeds, it would be worth the lecture you might get to know that you stood up for your rights and were able to call upon your parents for help. In fact, chances are your teacher won't report you. She'll be too busy worrying about herself and fearing that she may be in deep trouble. If she does report you, and your parents come down too hard on you, you might want to tell them that you had confidence that they would back you up in this situation, and you took the risk. You could then ask for mercy!!

–TEACHERS ARE NATURAL WORKAHOLICS–

Most teachers are workaholics, at least to some extent. They assign more work than students want, because they believe that it's good for the students. They feel, and rightly so, that once the work is done, students experience a sense of achievement that makes them feel good about themselves.

Teachers who give lots of work are really just doing their job—and doing it well. Remember: If it's more work for you, it's much more work for them, because they have to do the grading of all those exercises, papers, reports, and projects.

Teachers tell me that students will always complain, "It's too much work"; but in the end, miraculously, they do it. How? I guess they shorten their television and telephone time. Some may even choose not to work long hours at after-school jobs so that the schoolwork can get done. I say, do whatever it takes. Schoolwork comes first.

-SCHOOL IS YOUR "JOB"-

When you're a student, your priority has to be school, because school is your "work." It's your main job. What you do now in school will help to determine what you'll be doing for the rest of your life. The grades you get will, of course, influence which colleges you will get into, but more than that, the discipline you learn, the mental habits you form, will have a great influence on how successful you are in your chosen career.

If you learn to defer relaxation, such as watching television, and the material pleasures that require you to spend time on after-school jobs instead of homework, the self-discipline you put into practice in order to get your school-work done will carry over to your adult life. You'll be able to do twice as much as others, yet still have time for fun. (Don't misunderstand me. I'm all for after-school jobs. I'm only against them when they drain energy that should be spent on schoolwork.)

-THE INTOLERABLE WORKAHOLIC-

Some teachers do make unrealistic demands on high school students, piling on the assignments to the point where they cannot be completed in the time available, unless other coursework suffers. Some do this because they remember how much work they had when they were in high school and fear that standards are being lowered. They refuse to give in to what they see as the thinning out of education.

Other "workaholic" teachers overload their students because they are workaholics in their own daily lives, and they assume that others should be that way, too.

If you are in a situation where you are being asked to do work you cannot handle, you don't have to go under. First you have to determine whether the problem is the difficulty of the work or its volume. If it's the difficulty, you might want to try a private tutor. If you can't afford one, ask for free tutoring after school. (Speak to your teacher about it. All schools offer such help.)

My own daughter was having trouble with a difficult math course. The teacher was no help at all, advising her to face the fact—she just wasn't a math student. I hired a private tutor who told her she was talented in math and who helped her to understand things her teacher was unable to explain satisfactorily. End result—she passed the course, and with quite a respectable grade.

Another idea is to try to change classes. In most schools, there is more than one teacher offering a given course. Even though similar material may be covered, one teacher can make the work seem simple while another teacher can make it seem complicated. This is especially true in math.

The amount of work can also vary greatly from teacher to teacher, particularly in subjects like English and various courses in the humanities. For example, one teacher may require the reading of three outside books for reports, while another teacher may require only one. One teacher may give a hundred vocabulary words, while another may require only fifty, and one teacher may choose to teach three of Shakespeare's plays, while another teacher may teach only one plus two short novels. The length of homework assignments can also vary, sometimes by as much as an hour a night, depending upon your teacher.

Most chairpeople are wise enough to know which teacher would best fit your needs if you gave him or her a chance to help you. But you have to make the move. Department chairs are not mind readers. They are not going to walk into your room and ask, "Are you being overwhelmed by this class?" It's up to you to let them know about the problem.

Another solution if the work is too difficult is changing tracks. For example, if you're in the honors program, you can switch over to a regular program—at least in that one troublesome subject. It's better to drop an honors class in favor of a regular class and a respectable grade, than to get a failing grade or even a low passing grade.

Whether your problem teacher is a martinet, a work-aholic, or a combination of both, there's no need for you to fail a class or even to accept a low mark. If you think clearly and take action, you can make the best of the situation, and in the long run, you will have gained more than just a good grade. You will have gained the ability to deal with difficult people—a skill that you will be able to use time and again to make your life more pleasant, well after you graduate high school.

–REMINDERS–

1. A martinet is a strict disciplinarian or stickler for rigid regulations. Some teachers are martinets—and they're not going to change.

2. You can learn to cope with martinets if you analyze exactly what it is that makes them happy, and act accordingly.

3. Some martinets are more "martinet-ish" than others, but with self-control, you can handle even these.

4. If all your teacher wants of you is something minor—such as doing your notebook heading a certain way, writing on a certain size paper, or not chewing gum—why not give in? It's foolish to waste your energy trying

to change your teacher. Can you really teach an old dog new tricks?

5. If the work in a particular class is too difficult, try a private or after-school tutor.

6. If your teacher makes an extremely unfair demand, stand up for your rights. Ask a parent to come to school to obtain justice for you. Don't hesitate because you fear being reported for past offenses.

7. School is your "work"—your job—and should be your priority. It's worth sacrificing several television and telephone hours, and even cutting down on your after-school work hours, in order to do well.

8. If the class is too difficult no matter how hard you work or how much additional help you get, speak to your department chairperson about getting your class changed.

5

Sarcastic, Funny, or Insulting?

Have you ever been insulted by a sarcastic comment made by your teacher? For example, suppose you came to class a few minutes late one morning and quietly entered the room hoping not to draw attention to yourself, when suddenly the teacher exclaimed, "How nice of you to join us," and everyone laughed. How would you feel? Would you be angry with the teacher, or would you be able to laugh with the rest of the class even if you were a little embarrassed?

Teachers use sarcasm a lot. Most of the time, they don't mean to be insulting. They're just trying to be funny. Other times, however, they do intend to insult, or they go too far in a moment of anger without thinking of the consequences for you. In this chapter, we'll try to find out the difference between the two intentions and how to handle each of them.

–WHAT IS SARCASM?–

Sarcasm involves making fun of something or someone in a clever way. It is usually based on irony—a type of expression that emphasizes a point by stating the opposite of what is really meant. For example, Mrs. Smith, in referring to her student John, might say, "This brilliant student forgot his book." What she really means to say, of course, is, "John, you idiot, how could you forget your book?"

–THE DIFFERENCE BETWEEN FUNNY SARCASM AND INSULTING SARCASM–

Funny sarcasm makes you laugh and leaves you feeling stimulated, while insulting sarcasm leaves you feeling belittled, diminished, and angry. I asked teenagers to give me examples of humorous sarcasm used by teachers. Here's what they said.

> I handed in my assignment, and my teacher said, "I see your bird helped you with your homework." I asked, "What do you mean?" and he answered, "It looks like chicken scratches." I laughed.
>
> *Kim, 13*

> When my teacher asked me to go to the board to write the math problem, instead of calling me by my name, he said, "Vampira . . ." I thought it was funny, because I'm pale and have jet-black hair, and I wear blood-red lipstick. Everyone laughed.
>
> *Jennifer, 15*

> The teacher had put some work on the board and I raised my hand and asked, "Do we have to copy that?" He said, "No, I only want you to look at it, but make sure you sit there with your mouth open." We all cracked up.
>
> *Tony, 16*

The teacher always writes the homework on the board in the same spot, but I never look because I'm lazy, so I asked her, "What do we have to do for homework?" She says, "You have to twiddle your thumbs for a half hour." Then she starts circling her thumbs around each other and adds, "At least your hands will get some exercise, because Lord knows your brain doesn't. Ever think of looking at the homework section of the board, genius?" She's a joke.

Tommy, 17

The teacher had just explained how we had to do our term paper, and I raised my hand and asked her if it would count for the whole term. She said, "Hello. It's a term paper. It will count for the term. Any other intelligent questions?" I just smiled and thought, woops. I did it again. I didn't think before I spoke.

Jessica, 14

-IT'S FUNNY IF YOU'RE NOT OVERLY SENSITIVE-

The above examples of sarcasm were intended to make a point in a humorous way, and were taken in the spirit in which they were intended. Fortunately, none of these teenagers are overly sensitive, or they could have interpreted the comments as a personal attack.

For example, if Kim were touchy, she could have taken offense when the teacher said her handwriting resembled chicken scratches. Instead, she enjoyed the joke and probably went on to think, "He's right. My mother says the same thing."

Jennifer could easily have felt like dying of embarrassment when the teacher called her Vampira, and a less secure girl would have. But her teacher probably understands that Jennifer enjoys looking like "Vampira" and that she appreciates special attention—even when it's at her own expense.

Tony, Tommy, and Jessica all asked the kind of questions that drive teachers crazy. If there's one thing a teacher can't stand, it's a student wasting class time by asking a question with an obvious answer. For example, Tommy asked, "Do we have to copy that?", when everyone in the class knew that copying what was on the board was the daily routine.

Fortunately, these teachers were not too heavy-handed in their responses, and all three teens were also good-natured. They realized that they had failed to think before speaking, and when the teacher pointed this out in a humorous way, they were able to join in the laughter that followed. If they had been unable to lighten up and laugh at themselves, they might have felt that they had been humiliated.

–WHAT IF YOU CAN'T TAKE A JOKE?–

But what if your ego is rather fragile, or you're extremely sensitive and not able to laugh it off when you become the object of a teacher's humor? What do you do if the comment feels like a punch in the stomach, a slap in the face, or a stab in the heart—even though you know the teacher didn't mean it to have that effect?

Write the teacher a note, put it in a sealed envelope, and hand it to her after class; then run (because you're probably also a bit shy, too). The note could read something like this:

Dear Mrs. Smith:
I know you don't mean to insult me, but when you say things like [. . . .], the way you did the other day, it really hurts. I would appreciate it if you could please not put me on the spot that way any more, and I'll try not to give you any reason to do so.
Sincerely,
Your name

A note such as this is sure to work. I can't imagine a teacher in the world who would not go out of the way to avoid offending the writer of such a humble and sensitive plea in the future. As a matter of fact, many teachers would be so moved that they would apologize to the writer, and be very careful not to do anything to embarrass that student in the future.

–WHEN THE SARCASM IS OBVIOUSLY INSULTING–

Some teachers like to exercise their intelligence in the form of satire; they like to use a mild form of ridicule to expose stupidity, foolishness, or wrongdoing, and that's all well and good. However, what happens when teachers are downright cutting and derisive—when they seem to have contempt for you, and to enjoy making that contempt public? I asked teenagers to give me examples of situations in which teachers have offended them by making caustic remarks. Here's what they said:

I asked my teacher to explain the math problem for the second time, and he said, "My eight-year-old daughter understood that three years ago, but okay, here we go again." When a teacher does that it makes

me want to go back to what I was doing before—
cutting class every day.

Sandy, 15

The teacher had marked a vocabulary test and the
whole class got very low grades. He stood up in front
of the room and said, "You are the meaning of stupidity."

Valerie, 14

My science teacher always has a frown on his face—
he never smiles, and that especially makes me
gloomy. Then when I ask him a question, he'll say,
"If you have to ask me this, you'll never make it in
life." I don't think a teacher should be saying that to
a student. I can take it, but it could give someone
else a complex for the rest of her life.

Gloria, 14

I used a slang word, "ain't," and my teacher said,
"Is that how they speak at home?" I felt like throwing something at him. It was as if he was putting
down my family. Why can't he leave my family out
of it?

Don, 17

I cursed at the teacher, and she said to me, "Why
don't you tell it to your mother? I'm sure she would
appreciate it." Then when I complained about her
remark, she said, "I'm not insulting your mother. I'm
just saying, 'I'm sure your mother would never put
up with such language.' " But I know she was really
trying to say, "Why don't you curse your mother out
and not me."

Karen, 16

What we have here are frustrated teachers. They are wrong to insult the students just because they are having a hard time getting through to them; but being human, they also make mistakes at times. Let's analyze each situation and see if we can determine the exact "message" the teacher is giving the student.

In saying that three years ago his eight year old had already learned the math that fifteen-year-old Sandy can't learn today, the teacher is really asking, "Sandy, why are you so slow?" Obviously, he does not accept the fact that people learn different things at different rates, and has let his impatience get the better of him.

Of course it is painful for Sandy to be insulted this way. Yet, were she to realize that it is her teacher and not she who has the real problem (as a professional, he should understand and accept that people learn at different rates), she could brush aside his sarcasm and tell him after class that it really hurts to be insulted when you're trying to learn something. Chances are, he would get the message and check himself the next time he was tempted to make a similar comment. If not, Sandy could report him to the department chairperson.

When Valerie's teacher tells the class, "You are the meaning of stupidity," what he's really saying is, "I am frustrated because I don't know how to motivate you to study. I feel as if I'm failing as a teacher."

Don's teacher is something of a snob. What he's really saying is, "Your speech indicates that you come from an uncultivated family." If I were Don, I would speak to the teacher after class and ask him to leave my family out of his discussions with me. I think he would get the message.

Tired of being cursed at, Karen's teacher asks her why she doesn't talk that way to her mother. She probably meant to say that Karen should show the same respect in school that she does at home—not that she should show her mother the same disrespect she shows her teacher.

Karen, like many teenagers, is overly sensitive to the word "mother" and believes, in spite of the teacher's explanation, that the teacher is insulting her mother. If I were Karen, I would take the teacher at her word. Teachers are rarely interested in insulting people's parents. What they are interested in is being treated with a certain amount of respect.

–What Should You Do If Your Teacher Has Really Hurt Your Feelings?–

Most teachers know when they have stepped over the line and said something hurtful to a student, and this is to your advantage. If your teacher has said something to you that left you feeling put-down, angry, or hurt, you don't have to bury your emotions. You can instead bring things out in the open and clear the air.

Give yourself a day to cool off and then ask to speak to the teacher after class. Express yourself simply and without using accusatory words. Describe exactly how the teacher's words made you feel. "Mr. Jones, I felt like crying when you said that even an eight year old . . . ," or "Mrs. Smith, I wanted to put my fist through the wall when you called me retarded in front of the whole class." If there is anything you do like about the teacher, you might say so in passing in order to be more evenhanded in your complaint, even though the teacher did not pay *you* that courtesy: "I think you're a good teacher and I like you, but when you say things like that . . ."

The teacher will then do one of three things: (1) apologize, explaining that he or she was in a bad or frustrated mood but shouldn't have taken it out on you, (2) deny having meant to be insulting—saying something like, "Oh, I was just kidding," or (3) insult you again, saying something like, "Well, you *are* slow."

In the first case, accept the apology and be happy. In the second, accept the denial and be happy. Such a denial is a disguised form of apology, only the teacher is too embarrassed or afraid to admit that he was wrong. In the third case, give the teacher one more chance, and if another episode occurs, write down a description of the incident and report it to the department chairperson. You can be sure the chairperson will speak to the teacher about it. If by some chance it happens after that, report it again—and again and again until pressure from the chairperson causes the teacher to stop insulting the students. Although you can't be positive that such a change will be permanent—the teacher may just have a bad attitude—you can be sure of one thing: If you do nothing about the situation, nothing will change. You will just sit there and "stew," or end up telling the teacher off one day and getting into trouble. As difficult as it may seem to lodge such a complaint with the teacher or the teacher's supervisor, it's up to you to take action if you feel the sarcasm has gotten out of hand and you are upset by it.

–WHY WE'RE SARCASTIC— TEACHERS CONFESS–

The best way to find out why teachers are sarcastic is to go to the source. Here's what teachers had to say when asked why they are sarcastic to students.

I use jokes to motivate them. The kids appreciate my humor. They will come to me and say, "You know,

I tell my father what you say every night. You should be a comedian." I tell them, "I write my own lines."

Global history teacher, 13 years

I think the students relate to sarcasm. They pick up on it and enjoy it.

Algebra teacher, 7 years

I do it for fun, in a loving, kind way.

Reading teacher, 18 years

It's a safety hatch, an escape. Instead of blowing up, it defuses the situation. You have to have a sense of humor, otherwise you're dead.

Economics teacher, 14 years

They'll make some outrageous comment, and I'll let them have it.

English teacher, 20 years

When I'm sarcastic and nasty, usually it's because they have said something I dislike and insulted me and set me off.

English teacher, 10 years

I make acidic comments. It's not one of my finer qualities. It's my nature.

American history teacher, 9 years

I came into teaching with high expectations, and when I see something that's very disappointing (which is often), I respond with sarcasm.

English teacher, 22 years

Teachers are sarcastic for many reasons. Some use sarcasm for fun. They like their own wit and enjoy being thought of as comedians. If humor is good-natured, and the students appreciate it, it can lighten things up and take some of the drudgery out of both teaching and learning.

Other teachers use sarcasm to make a point. It's their way of saying something serious in a funny way so that the students will get the message without having it hammered into them.

Still other teachers use sarcasm as an outlet for their frustrations. However, they admit, the sarcasm sometimes gets out of hand, and when it does, they are not proud of themselves.

Can we forgive them? Perhaps we can. Let's face it: It isn't easy to be kind and gentle all the time when you're dealing with over a 150 teenagers every day. When pushed too far, most of us can get pretty nasty. In fact, I often ask my classes how many of them would consider teaching teenagers as a career, and they invariably reply: "No way." When I ask why not, they tell me that they could never put up with what we face without hauling off and punching someone.

Teachers have a responsibility to use self-control, and most of the time, they do. But if at times your teacher gets a little nasty, perhaps you can forgive him or her—just this once or twice. What do you think?

-REMINDERS-

1. Sarcasm is making fun of something in a clever way. It often involves irony, a type of humorous expression in which the person speaking says the exact opposite of what he really means—to emphasize a point.

2. Many teachers use sarcasm as a form of humor. No harm is intended; however, a very sensitive person may

take certain remarks too personally and become insulted.

3. Some teachers are insulting in their use of sarcasm. Such teachers may be frustrated because they feel that they're not getting through to you, and angry because they do not know how to do a better job of teaching.

4. If you feel offended when your teacher is sarcastic with you, give yourself a day to cool off and then explain your feelings in a note or speak to your teacher after class.

5. If the teacher continues to insult you and hurt your feelings even after you have explained yourself, you don't have to be a victim. Talk to the department chairperson, who will then speak to the teacher about it.

6

The Eyesore, Earsore, Nosesore, Etc.

Her name was Miss Ross. Her hair was curly blond, and like brillo. She would always wear her favorite shoes, which were pink. It looked as if she had had those pink things ever since she started teaching.

Tanya, 15

The names of the teachers discussed in this chapter have been changed—to save them from embarrassment. Did you ever have a teacher who was an offense to the eye, one that you couldn't stand looking at for more than two minutes, much less forty? You're not alone. When I asked teenagers to give me examples of teachers that drove them crazy, most of them had at least one story to tell about a teacher who either looked bad, smelled bad, sounded bad, or did something bad.

But before I get myself in trouble with my colleagues, let me say that the teachers described in this chapter are the exception and not the rule. Well, if that's the case, then how come I heard so many stories? When you think of it, most teenagers have dealt with at least fifty teachers by the time they are fifteen years old, and about ninety by the time they are eighteen years old. (You have one teacher per year through grade six, and after that, you have six to eight teachers per term, or twelve to sixteen per year, right?) If that's the case, even if every teenager only had one teacher that fits into this chapter, that teacher, one out of fifty to ninety, would still be quite the exception, and not the rule.

Why do some teachers wear the same outfit three times in one week? How could a teacher not know that she is in desperate need of deodorant? Is it possible a teacher doesn't realize he swallows his words so badly that you can't hear a word he's saying, and that other teachers are oblivious to the fact that they are screaming at the top of their lungs? In this chapter, we'll talk about teachers who are an offense to the eye, the nose, and the ear, and we'll try to understand why. We'll also talk about how to survive if you encounter one of these teachers.

–HE WORE THOSE BOOTS EVEN IN HUNDRED-DEGREE WEATHER. . . .–

You have to sit there every day. You're a captive audience. And what do you see?

> She had no shape—her back looked like her front. There were no arms. She was like a pencil up and down. You could read the newspaper through her. If she's married, her husband's got to be out of his mind. It looks like she has on a wedding band—but it couldn't be, could it?
>
> *Alice, 14*

Her colors never matched. She would wear a black dress with a brown belt and a green scarf and navy blue shoes.

Keisha, 16

He wore these old Pumas from the 1950s. Maybe they used to be white at one time, but now they're all brown and raggedy, and the leather was coming out on the bottom—on the side. The laces were black. I mean *black*. Another thing . . . you could smell his sneakers from a mile away.

John, 16

He wore the same pants and shirt every day. His shirts were always short-sleeved, and you had to look at his hairy arms.

Roxanne, 13

He wore those same boots with the run-down heels every day, even in one hundred-degree weather.

Vickey, 16

When my teacher goes out of the room for anything, he takes his briefcase with him as if we were going to steal something from him. But the worst thing is, he always has some white stuff at the corners of his mouth.

Paul, 15

This teacher burps and picks his nose right in front of the class—then acts like nothing's wrong.

Andy, 17

Sometimes my teacher would take a tissue and stick it under her armpit inside her dress and then take it out and smell it. She was disgusting. And she did smell bad, too.

Aimee, 13

Platform heels and bell-bottom pants—I think she's in a time warp. I guess as long as she's doing her job, that's what counts. After all, she's not being paid to look good.

Marcia, 15

My bio teacher eats a boiled egg and rye bread, and then drinks some water or club soda in a big, fat test tube with about ten pieces of ice. It stinks up the whole classroom.

Roger, 18

He wears this old brown suit with missing buttons and the pants hanging down too low. He's always pulling them up. The cuffs are all raggedy from dragging on the floor. I think we should take up a collection for him. I mean, nobody could be that poor.

Frankie, 15

Why do teachers look the way these teachers do? Well, first of all, some of them can't help themselves. For example, it isn't fair to fault a teacher for being skinny. After all, what should Alice's teacher do, hide her shape under a sack, or pad her buttocks? Apparently, as Alice notes, she's married. Wonder of wonders. Someone actually accepted her the way she is. Just goes to show that looks aren't all that matter.

There are always going to be fat teachers, skinny teachers, not-so-good-looking teachers, elderly teachers, short teachers, and tall teachers. They come in every size, age, and shape—and so do teens for that matter. So I guess we'll have to try to forgive everyone if they're not exactly model material.

-THEY COULD USE A COURSE IN FASHION DESIGN-

Some teachers certainly could stand improvement in the quality and style of their dress: Keisha's teacher who mismatches her colors, Marcia's who wears platform heels, Frankie's who wears a baggy, frayed, buttonless suit, Roxanne's who wears short-sleeved shirts that reveal his hairy arms, and John's who never seems to change out of his old Pumas, are all examples of this problem.

Did you ever stop to think that some teachers may be poor? It's possible, you know. As mentioned before, they are far from the most highly paid of all professionals. Some of them have more than one child to put through college, others have aging parents to support, and others have child support and alimony and debts to pay. Even with a second job, sometimes ends just don't meet.

Also, some teachers may have other priorities. They may have decided to buy a house in spite of the gigantic mortgage payments and now may have to spend the major part of their salary on that, or they may feel that clothing is not as important as travelling or collecting antiques. Who knows? It's not for you or anyone to judge.

-SOME TEACHERS HAVE QUIRKS-

A quirk is an oddity or a strange mannerism. Some teachers are peculiar or odd, even a bit eccentric. They don't have their "axis" in the center, so to speak. Such people are slightly "off base," a departure from the norm. They're not crazy, just a little strange. Vickey's teacher who wears boots even in one hundred-degree weather, and Roger's teacher who drinks water with ice cubes from a thick test tube, are examples. And why should this surprise you? Aren't there some eccentrics in every profession? Why should teaching be any different?

–THEY DON'T REALIZE THEY HAVE AN AUDIENCE–

Some teachers apparently lose sight of the fact that when they stand in front of the room, the spotlight is on them. They seem to be oblivious to the fact that unlike many office workers, they cannot fade into the woodwork.

Being a teenager, this is likely to shock you, but believe it or not, some people rarely look in the mirror. In addition, some people do not have a full-length mirror in their homes, so they don't really get to see the whole picture—how bad they really look.

And even when they do look in the mirror, some people don't see what the world sees. They see something completely different. Why? They've gotten so used to the sight of themselves that no matter how raggedy or mismatched they are, they don't register it. (The same goes for body odor, by the way. If you smell yourself long enough, you get used to the odor. Others, of course, notice it right away.)

Some teachers are overly practical. They think nothing of wearing the same thing every day and care less what they look like. Their only concern is having something to cover their bodies. Roxanne's teacher doesn't worry that his hairy arms are unattractive, and he's not interested in matters of style. Fashion is the last thing on his mind. Since he doesn't even look in a mirror, you can be sure he doesn't check the store windows, newspapers, or fashion magazines to see what other people are wearing. As long as he's got something on his back, he's happy.

Paul's teacher, who spits as he talks, does so out of habit and is probably unaware that he's doing it. Even if he did look in the mirror, he would get no information on how he looks when he's speaking, since we don't usually talk to our own mirror images. As for why he takes his briefcase with him every time he leaves the room—apparently this wise man has learned from experience (his own or that of other teachers) to guard his property. In most schools, things are taken, either out of mischief or as a result of theft. You should see the teachers in my school guarding their purses, keys, delaney books, you name it. It's so obsessive with us, and with good reason, that it's become an ongoing joke. Teachers walk around the building clutching their purses and constantly checking for their keys, even though they just saw them a minute ago.

Why is this behavior offensive to some teens? They interpret it as saying "I don't trust you." But it doesn't mean that at all. The message there, and it's nothing personal, is, "I'm not taking any chances. I have enough troubles already without losing my briefcase, my purse, or my keys."

The teachers with the horrible personal habits aren't difficult to explain either. When alone, people do all sorts of things they wouldn't do in public, but most people have a built-in "check" system and automatically modify their behavior when others are around. Andy's teacher who picks his nose and burps in front of the class, and Aimee's teacher who puts a tissue under her dress to check her armpit and then smells it, for some reason or other, have short-circuited check systems. They behave as if no one is watching them.

You've no doubt seen strangers do equally offensive things in the street, on public transportation, and even in company, at parties. Such people are daydreaming, forgetting for a moment that they are visible to those around them. Apparently some teachers daydream or forget themselves in this way, too, even though they are in front of the class.

In other circumstances, a teacher's offensiveness is a statement. It may be an unconscious way of saying, "Stay away from me. Leave me alone." In such cases, the offensive dress or behavior serves as a barrier between the teacher and the rest of the world—especially students.

"But doesn't anyone tell these teachers what they're doing or how they look?" you might ask. Perhaps one or two brave souls have ventured to say something, but maybe not. After all, most people don't want to take the chance of insulting someone else. They don't want to hurt or incite the person. We've all heard the story of the messenger who got his head chopped off just because he delivered bad news to the king!!!

–NO ONE CAN UNDERSTAND HIM!!!–

I don't know who he thinks he's talking to, but when Mr. Allen teaches, he faces the board and talks to himself so almost nobody can hear him.

Dave, 14

My Spanish teacher can't speak English. Why did they hire him? He doesn't pronounce his words correctly, and then he gets mad when you don't know what he's talking about. Someone should tell him to go back to school.

Nicole, 16

Unfortunately, after college graduation, teachers are not required to take courses in speech or public speaking. How a teacher speaks to a group ends up being a matter of innate ability. Some teachers are "naturals" at it and automatically project their voices, enunciate their words, and maintain proper voice level. Others, however, need lots of help in this area, but probably don't receive any.

It would be nice if all school systems offered free public speaking courses to teachers; but as it stands, it costs at least $500.00 for any worthwhile course, a lot of money for most teachers. In addition, even if they don't care about the money, they are usually so overworked, that unless forced to take the course by way of requirement, they'd rather not spend the time.

If you can't hear your teacher, however, you have a right to complain. For example, every time Dave's teacher talks to the board, Dave could raise his hand and say, "Excuse me, we can't hear you. Could you please turn around?" Not easy, you say. I agree, but what choice do you have? If you sit there and do nothing, you, and not the teacher, will be the one to lose out. Some teachers will even appreciate your asking, since it does imply a desire on your part to hear what they say.

If Nicole is in a Spanish class, how can she learn when her teacher can't speak English well enough to be understood? Nicole has a right to complain to the department chairperson. The department head will then either get help for that teacher or hire someone else. Some things are just not fair to the students and cannot be tolerated.

–STOP SCREAMING!!!–

Some teachers yell at the top of their lungs, for no apparent reason.

If you take aspirins to get rid of a headache, you take a dose of Mr. Singer's voice to give you one. You walk into the class, and immediately he's screaming, "Get into your seats, there's work on the board." I mean, you haven't even done anything wrong yet, and already he's yelling. He keeps that up all period long. "Why didn't you do the homework? Hurry up with that reading assignment. Stop talking. You're in the wrong seat. Behave like a gentleman." It never stops. Doesn't the man realize that we are not deaf and that he could say the same thing in a normal voice?

William, 17

I'm actually scared of Mrs. Johnson—and when I come to think of it, it's her fierce, loud, shrill voice. If there were hound dogs in our class, they would all sit up and howl at the sound of her voice. I think she just loves to hear herself scream. I walk on tiptoes just not to offend her, because I know the minute I do something wrong, she will raise the roof with her voice. Everyone knows about her, because you can hear her yelling on the third floor, and she teaches on the fourth floor.

Kim, 14

My teacher doesn't scream when she's angry, she just plain screams when she talks. I don't believe she realizes it. One time I said, "Mrs. Thomas, could you please lower your voice? We can hear you. You talk too loud." She looked embarrassed and lowered her voice for about one minute, but the volume gradually increased to its normal level, and I was holding my ears again.

Betsy, 16

I can certainly sympathize with these students. Teachers yell for different reasons. Apparently, both Mr. Singer and

Mrs. Johnson are frustrated and angry with student behavior and have found a way to vent those feelings. Unfortunately for both teacher and student, nothing but more anger and frustration is accomplished this way.

Betsy's teacher has a different problem altogether. She doesn't realize that she's yelling. It's the way she naturally speaks. Nevertheless, it's a problem to students who have to listen to her for some forty-odd minutes a day.

If your teacher yells incessantly, for whatever the reason may be, there are several possible courses you can take. 1) You can write a kind note, expressing your enjoyment of the class and then telling how unfortunate it is that the volume of his (her) voice takes away from that enjoyment, even to the point of giving you a headache. 2) You can speak to the teacher after class. 3) You can band together with a few other students and speak to the department chairperson, making sure that you emphasize that you are not trying to get the teacher in trouble, but just want him (her) to get a grip on the problem.

There is no guarantee that any of this will work. If you try it and nothing happens, it's up to you to decide how important it is. If the yelling will eventually cause you to cut class, to tune the teacher out, and to eventually get lower grades or to fail the class, then you owe it to yourself to do something drastic about it. You may want to ask for a class change and if you are refused, to bring your parent in, who will, I assure you, cause action to be taken on your behalf.

Remember. It's your life. If you find yourself in a situation where you know that if you don't take action, you will pay the price, and you still do nothing, you have no one to blame but yourself.

–SOME BAD BREATH
CAN'T BE CURED
WITH MOUTHWASH–

This teacher would always talk in my face, I mean, if you were anywhere near her, she would practically jump on top of you—and, like, you would keep backing away. If you were near a window, you might go flying out just to get away from her. Her breath smelled bad, and I mean bad.

Carol, 15

Perhaps such a teacher could find the solution to her problem in a bottle of mouthwash. The class could chip in for a few bottles and put one in her desk drawer every week until she got the message. If the message still didn't get through, the only other solution is to do what Carol did—back up!

Before you condemn the teacher for not dealing with a condition that seems simple to cure, remember that it's possible her problem cannot be solved with mouthwash. Some people have a stomach disorder that causes them to have perpetually bad breath. These cases can sometimes be helped by medication or a change of diet. A gift of mouthwash obviously would not be an antidote to the problem. However, it would at least help to alert them to the situation and perhaps prompt them to seek medical help.

–TAKE A SHOWER!–

Did you ever have a friend who needed deodorant? Did you tell her about it? Probably not. It's embarrassing to confront people about body odor or other such intimate problems, and it's also risky—they may take offense. What then can you, a student, do if you have a teacher who needs deodorant? You can either keep your distance or chance a kind—and anonymous—note to that effect.

Dear Mrs. Smith:
We think you're a great teacher, so we think we owe it to you to help you with something that you may be unaware of. You need deodorant. We hope you will accept this as a kindness rather than as an insult. If any one of us had the problem, we would be glad if someone let us know.

Sincerely,
Some class members

If I received such a note, I would be very embarrassed, but the first chance I got, I'd run out and buy two bottles of deodorant and keep one of them in my school locker for insurance purposes—just in case, for some reason, I forgot to apply deodorant at home one morning.

Some teachers, however, would not appreciate such a note. They might see it as an obnoxious joke, or as student hostility. Like many people, such teachers are defensive and find it difficult to face their failings. It's easier to run away from unpleasant truths than to face them, especially if that revelation will require change. In addition, some people are comfortable the way they are and will not change, no matter how clear matters are made to them. They are set in their ways—whether or not these ways are offensive to others.

How do some teachers get away with smelling bad year after year, you may wonder? An office worker could never get away with it because his or her co-workers would not tolerate having to put up with the odor in close quarters for eight hours a day. Students, on the other hand, only have to endure the odor for forty minutes. When the bell rings, they're out of there, so it's less likely that any of them would go to the administration to lodge a complaint.

–THE FINAL SAY ON EYESORES, EARSORES, AND NOSESORES–

What then is there to say in the end about these noxious types? No one ever died from seeing something "ugly" (think of all the horror movies you've seen) or smelling something bad (you fill in the example here). If it doesn't bother you that much, you can just tough it out and be glad that all of your teachers don't look that way, sound that way, or smell that way. If it does bother you a lot, you can always try subtle ways of letting the teacher know, or report the problem to the department chairperson. If you don't, chances are, no one else will, and the offense will continue forever.

–REMINDERS–

1. Not all teachers are fashion conscious. In fact, some rarely look in the mirror, much less in store windows or fashion magazines.

2. Some teachers dress poorly because they *are* poor. Others have different priorities for how to spend their hard-earned money.

3. Some teachers are oblivious to the fact that the spotlight is on them when they are teaching, so they behave in

an offensive manner, doing things that people ordinarily do in private when no one can see them.

4. Some teachers dress or behave in strange ways because they are eccentric. There are strange people or oddballs in every profession: Teaching is no exception.

5. If your teacher's speech is inaudible, you have a right to raise your hand and say, "Can you speak more clearly? I can't hear you."

6. If you can't understand your teacher, by all means report it to your chairperson, who will either get help for that teacher or put you in another class with someone you can understand.

7. If your teacher has bad breath or body odor, you might try writing her a discreet, kind, anonymous note, or getting together with classmates and leaving a bottle of the appropriate substance in her desk drawer until she gets the message.

8. Some people are comfortable with themselves even though they cause offense to others and will not change no matter how clear matters are made to them.

9. Teachers such as those who are mentioned in this chapter continue to be the way they are because they are rarely reported to the administration. If you encounter one of them, you can decide to either live and let live, or do something about it. The choice is yours—and either one is good.

7

The Soap Opera Star

The soap opera star, as you might have guessed, is the teacher who likes to talk incessantly about his or her personal life, at the expense of teaching. At first, the class finds it interesting. After all, it does break the monotony of the daily routine of reading that book, answering those questions, or writing that composition. However, after a while, even the not-so-serious students begin to feel cheated: "I thought we were here to learn. . . ," they say to themselves. "Why is the teacher wasting so much time talking about . . . ?"

Why do some teachers go overboard talking about their personal lives? Should teachers ever relate personal experiences to the students, and if so, where should they draw the line? How do teenagers feel about teachers who never talk about their personal lives?

In this chapter, we'll talk about the "soap opera star," the well-meaning teacher who falls into the trap of forgetting that he or she is in the classroom to teach you the subject.

If anything, most teachers do not share enough of their personal lives with their students, so it's important to realize that the examples discussed here are by far the exception and not the rule, even though you probably will encounter one or two such examples during your school year.

–EVERYONE KNOWS ALL ABOUT HER DIVORCE. . . .–

I asked teens to give me examples of teachers who talked too much about their personal lives—to the point where it made them feel either uncomfortable (because they were embarrassed by the revelations), or cheated (because the teacher was wasting too much class time). They had plenty to say on the subject, though one student did seem to have found the experience amusing.

My teacher was going through a divorce, and everyone knew it, because that's all she talked about. It was an economics class, and no matter what we were discussing, she would go off about how unfair the economic system is to women, and how her husband is trying to cheat her out of what is rightfully hers.

Joanne, 16

I loved Mrs. Reis. We got to know all about her boyfriends. It wasn't that she didn't teach, because she did, but somehow it always got around to her life and her many boyfriends. Too bad she didn't give the tests on her boyfriends. I would have gotten a hundred.

Tracy, 15

Whenever we talk about a certain country, my social studies teacher goes off. He tells us all about his travels, and by the time he gets through, the bell is ringing and we still haven't talked about the assignment.

I liked it much better last year when I had Mr. Jones. We really learned a lot from him.

Judy, 16

It was about a month into the term when Mrs. Stone got pregnant. From then on, all you heard about was morning sickness, backaches, and baby names. After a while, when she started to talk, the whole class would yawn.

William, 14

Why do teachers talk to their classes about their personal lives? If they're going through a severe crisis, such as a divorce, their minds are dominated by the problem. They feel the way you would if the love of your life were threatening to break up with you—only worse.

"But a teacher should be able to put aside personal problems until after school," you may rightfully argue. "We don't get to talk about ourselves in class." Of course they "should," and fortunately, most do. But other teachers are not as self-controlled.

Some teachers, such as Tracy's, speak out of turn because of a lack of self-discipline and the inability to draw the line between appropriate and inappropriate teacher-student communication. They misuse their students, placing them in the role of close friends or "confidants."

It's easy enough for an outgoing teacher to fall into this trap. Teenagers are usually non-judgmental, interested listeners. How wonderful it must feel for Tracy's teacher to look forward to going to class the next day and tell her students the latest development in her romantic life. The only problem is, as Tracy suggests, the students learn more about the teacher's personal business than they do about the subject. A detailed knowledge of Mrs. Reis's boyfriend won't help them in their future lives.

William's social studies teacher likes to share travel experiences that relate to the lesson on hand, and this is fine. However, sometimes he forgets himself and gets carried away talking about his wonderful memories. Why doesn't he check himself and save his reminiscing for his friends? Perhaps he doesn't have many friends—and those he does have may be too busy with their own lives to listen to him. At least here, in his own classroom, he has a ready audience—and a captive one at that. His students cannot get up and excuse themselves, saying, "I have to go now," as a social acquaintance could. They must sit there and listen.

Other teachers, such as Judy's, talk endlessly about their personal lives because they are excited about an upcoming event. It's okay for teachers to share their joy with their students. There's no need for Ms. Pregnant to completely silence herself about her condition. All she has to do is talk less about it.

–WHAT CAN YOU DO WHEN A TEACHER DOESN'T TEACH?–

What can you do if your teacher continually digresses, and you feel you're missing important work? You can bring her back to reality by politely interrupting and asking a question about the lesson.

If the digression begins right at the start of the class, and ten minutes have gone by and the lesson has still not started, you can break in with a question about the homework, asking something like, "How much time do we have to do the assignment?" Such questions will help the teacher to realize that she has been wasting too much time with personal talk.

If you're in the middle of a class discussion, and the teacher goes off on a tangent, you can break in by raising your hand and asking a specific question about the book you are discussing: "Mrs. Ryan, could you please explain what is meant on page 63, the third paragraph?"

The teacher will not become angry because you are changing the subject. How could she? If anything, she will be slightly embarrassed, but grateful to you for reminding her to get back to business.

–WHAT IF YOUR EFFORTS TO GET THE TEACHER BACK ON TRACK FAIL?–

But what should you do if raising your hand and asking questions doesn't work—if your teacher *still* spends most of the time digressing, and you feel as if you're not learning anything in that class? There are, actually, several things you can do.

Try writing the teacher a signed note, expressing your feelings honestly, but politely. Be sure to begin the note in a complimentary way. You may want to start with something like, ". . . I really enjoy your class. You're always so cheerful, and the subject matter is so interesting. But I feel we miss out on a lot of work, because you sometimes get carried away talking about things unrelated to the lesson. . . ."

Most teachers do not plan to spend endless time discussing their personal lives and are embarrassed when they realize that they have been doing just that. If anything, they will appreciate your alerting them to the fact that they have been digressing.

But what if nothing changes after the note, and you still feel as if you're not going to learn a thing in that class? You guessed it. Speak to the department chairperson. And don't worry about getting the teacher in trouble. Chairpeople are there to help teachers, not to condemn them. Very often a little talk from a higher authority will set things straight. If that doesn't work, you can always go to the chairperson and request a class change.

–WHERE SHOULD THE LINE BE DRAWN?–

Most teachers are well aware of how far to go when discussing their personal lives with the students. They say:

> When something in the lesson relates to a personal experience, I'll talk about it. For example, we were learning about map scales and I told my class that I took my family camping in North Carolina, and that we almost got lost because I misread the map scale. But that's about as personal as I get.
>
> *Social studies teacher, 21 years*

> I told the students about my brother's drug problem because it related to a character in a novel we were reading. I wanted to show them that people from every walk of life can have these problems—even teachers' families.
>
> *Health ed teacher, 8 years*

> I told them that in my family no one expected me to achieve anything. My cousin was expected to succeed—I was not. But I ended up becoming a teacher, and he became a drifter. So, I point out, "Don't give up on yourself even if people don't believe in you."
>
> *World history teacher, 25 years*

> I do it a little bit—not too much, and never about sex.
>
> *English teacher, 5 years*

These kids are thirsty to be treated as adults. We don't give them enough credit. They respond very positively when you talk about your life—your traumatic experiences, your victories, your anger, your frustration, and so on.

Art teacher, 15 years

I tell them little things. For example, they know I like Michael Jackson, and whenever he's appearing somewhere or there's some news about him, a student will come and tell me. I draw the line when it comes to interfering with getting the work done.

Math teacher, 18 years

As you can see, most teachers agree that speaking about their personal lives is appropriate when it applies directly to the lesson, when it helps to make them appear more human, or offers inspiration to their students. In fact, teenagers find it difficult to form a bond with teachers who *never* talk about their personal lives. They say:

They seem cold—you wonder what's behind the mask. They're also a little scary. You don't feel free to really talk to them, because you can't trust them.

Pete, 16

When they act like it's all business, they give the impression that they're just doing a job—you know, in it for the paycheck at the end of the week, and that's all.

Tricia, 15

If all a teacher does is stick to what's in the book, you feel like you're being taught by a robot and not a real person.

Robby, 14

I'd rather have a crazy teacher who's fun than a straight teacher who is afraid to let down his hair.

Zoie, 13

Teenagers like it when teachers reveal themselves, and in fact feel threatened and alienated from teachers who refuse to disclose their human side. It's clear that the ideal teacher would reveal just enough and no more—and at the right time. But if your teacher is doing something that is less than perfect, it's up to you to decide whether or not that teacher's imperfection merits action—and then, how much action. Maybe you'll just want to grin and bear it. It's up to you.

–REMINDERS–

1. Some teachers talk too much about their personal lives, because they're going through a crisis and find comfort in "getting it off their chest."

2. Since students are a captive audience, it may be tempting for teachers who don't ordinarily have ready listeners in friends and acquaintances to take advantage of the situation.

3. Usually, teenagers are not as judgmental as adults and are quite sympathetic. Therefore, a teacher who has problems may be tempted to share them with students.

4. Some teachers start out by telling a personal anecdote that is related to the lesson, but then get carried away. They may welcome an effort on your part to return to the subject.

5. If your teacher is spending too much time talking about things unrelated to the lesson, you can bring the focus back to the subject by asking a question about the lesson or the homework.

6. If you feel that you're not learning what you should be because your teacher is wasting too much class time, write him a friendly note. Most teachers don't realize the extent to which they "digress," and most would probably be grateful for your interest.

7. While students feel uncomfortable when teachers talk incessantly about their personal lives, they're equally unhappy when teachers tell them nothing at all about themselves. They feel it makes teachers appear cold and inhuman. So try to make allowances if your teachers err in one direction or another. It's hard to find the right balance.

8

It's Not Fair!!!

Are teachers unfair? If not, why are they always being accused? If so, what are they unfair about? According to teenagers, they're unfair about lots of things, not just marks. Teenagers complain that teachers have "pets" as well as "whipping boys" (and girls), make false accusations, punish the entire class for the misdeeds of one or two students, call on a student when he doesn't have his hand up, refuse to review for tests, change seats at will, lower marks for misbehavior, give homework on Fridays, and so on.

In this chapter we'll discuss all of the above, and more. We'll also suggest ways to either live with the unfair treatment or, if it's serious enough, change it.

–TEACHER'S PET AND TEACHER'S WHIPPING BOY–

Some teachers have "pets," and at the same time have the opposite—people they pick on, known as "whipping boys."

My English teacher was not right. She liked this one kid Michael, and every time he gave an answer, no matter how stupid it was, she would smile and say, "Very good, Michael." But if someone else would have given the same answer, she would probably have made a face, as if to say, "How could you be so ignorant?" It's just not fair.

Tina, 17

My Spanish teacher gave me an 85 on the first report card, a 75 on the second, and a 70 on the third. It kept getting lower, and I know why. In the first marking period, I was really quiet. When I got used to the new school, I started talking to kids in the class, and I wouldn't always volunteer to go to the board any more. She kept lowering my mark just because I was acting like a normal teenager and not everybody's little pet.

Yvette, 16

My computer teacher didn't like me because when my brother was in her class, he had a big fight with her and was expelled from school, so when I went to the school, she took it all out on me.

Tanya, 14

Mrs. Roslyn hated me because I spoke my mind freely. She treated me like an outsider, so I didn't want to come to class any more.

Stanley, 15

This teacher was a real grouch and she couldn't stand the way I giggle when I laugh. I'm a happy person, and I laugh a lot, so she was always yelling at me, "Erica, stop that giggling. You're not five years old anymore." After a while she embarrassed me so much I started cutting, and I failed the class.

Erica, 13

The fact is, some teachers do have favorites, and some of them make no effort to hide it. Of course it's annoying to sit there, day after day, and watch your teacher fawn over someone while you are ignored. It's twice as annoying if the teacher makes a fuss over someone who isn't half as good a student as you are while your work has gone unnoticed. Tina doesn't say whether or not she feels her mark was fair, so I assume that the teacher's attitude did not carry over into the grades (as in cases we'll discuss later). If this is so, the best thing for Tina to do is ignore it, or watch it as if it were a TV show. It's not costing Tin a anything if Michael gets special treatment, is it?

Let's face the facts. You can't "win em" all, and Tina hasn't won this one—Michael has. Maybe next time Tina will win the teacher's favor, and then others may resent her. The wheel of fortune turns. Learn to live and let live. Realize that people's personalities naturally interact in different ways. It's normal for us to enjoy being around one person more than another. If a teacher is unable to hide her preference for someone in the class, it's not the end of the world. As long as she isn't picking on you or grading you unfairly—no problem. Just do your work and get your grade. End of story.

Yvette, however, whose mark has gone down every marking period, does feel that her teacher's attitude toward her has negatively affected her grade. She complains that her teacher is unfairly lowering her grade because she has become a normal teenager and is no longer quiet and docile. But if you read between the lines, you can see that it's unlikely that Yvette is doing the same quality work she was doing before. For example, she seldom goes to the board, and she talks to her friends (probably while the teacher is teaching). Her declining classwork may be the reason for her falling grades, and she may also be learning less because she's paying less attention. If, however, Yvette believes that her grade average, classwork included, is the same or higher than the last time, she owes it to herself to be shown in black and white exactly why her end-of-term mark is lower. She can politely ask to see a record of her grades. We'll talk about this in detail later in the chapter.

–SHE THINKS I'M MY BROTHER–

Tanya's teacher seems to have fallen into the trap of making faulty assumptions. She's had a negative experience with Tanya's brother, so she assumes she will also have trouble with Tanya. Her fear causes her to react negatively toward Tanya. Naturally, Tanya resents this. If something isn't said to clear the air, before long Tanya will probably tell the teacher off and bring on the very thing the teacher expects—an incident.

If you're in a situation where the teacher is behaving as if you are some member of your family who has been a troublemaker in the past, set her straight right from the beginning by having a talk with her in private. You can say something like, "I've always had problems because of . . . Teachers tend to take his bad behavior out on me. It really hurts me when they do that. Do you think you could help me and give me a chance to prove myself instead of blaming me for what someone else did?" Most teachers would quickly realize their mistake and apologize. They would in fact probably go out of the way to give you a fair shake from that day on.

-PERSONALITY CONFLICTS-

Stanley is the victim of a personality conflict. Some teachers are threatened by outspoken students because they are "more work" than the quiet, submissive types. Other teachers are annoyed by quiet, submissive students, because they are not as much fun to teach. Some teachers love a student with a ready joke and appreciate wit and humor when they see it. Others would label such a student as a "class clown" and make that student's life miserable.

It would be wonderful if everyone would appreciate us for what we are. Unfortunately, the reality is our "raw" selves are not always accepted with delight by others, and if they're the ones in power, we have to adjust our personalities to theirs—that is, if we plan to succeed in the very real world we live in.

"Ridiculous," you say. "I'm not going to be a phoney." Well, it isn't really being a phoney at all; it's being smart. Successful people are those who have learned to do such tuning in. That's what communication is all about.

So what can you do to make sure that yours won't be the personality your teacher "can't stand?" The answer is simple: Evaluate your audience. Think of it as market research. Your market is the teacher, and the product you're trying to sell is yourself. The self doesn't change, but the packaging can if necessary. If you can tell that your style is not going over very well with your teacher, why not alter your style to suit the situation—just for forty minutes a day. When you're with your friends, you can "let her rip" and enjoy the fact that you are flexible enough to change the outer package according to circumstances without ever compromising the inner self.

-I CAN'T STAND
THAT GIGGLING-

Erica's teacher can't stand giggling. It gets on her nerves. Gum chewing bothers me. Someone else abhors foot tapping. "Not fair," you say. "You teachers are just old grouches." Well, different things do annoy different people. Don't you find that to be true even among your friends and family?

Instead of taking it personally and viewing the teacher's dislike of her giggle as dislike of her, Erica would be wise to control her laugh and keep going to class. To take the tension out of the situation, she might say something like, "I know what you mean about my giggle. It drives my mother crazy, too. I'll try to control it." Just saying something like this can be a great comfort to the teacher, because it will indicate to her that the student has gotten the message and doesn't think she's an ogre. She may also respect such a student for being honest and generous enough to admit that other people—even the student's own mother—have complained about the giggle, too.

Why start cutting a class just because you think the teacher is picking on you? You're the only loser there, because you'll be the one repeating the course next semester, or going to summer school. Isn't it better to straighten things out so that you get the course over and done with? Even if the "attitude" persists right up until the last day of class, so what? You don't have to win a popularity contest with that teacher. You just have to control yourself so that you can pass the course. The fact is, in life, you can and will accomplish many things whether or not everyone involved likes you. Just continue to pursue your goal and try not to make the situation worse by provoking people.

-VEDRAL'S BELIEVE IT OR NOT: TEACHERS CAN AND DO LOWER MARKS FOR BEHAVIOR-

If your teacher is picking on you because something you do annoys her, why don't you stop doing it? Is it that you enjoy provoking the teacher just to see her reaction? Is it sheer stubbornness—you don't want her to win? Forget it. Whether it's snapping gum, tapping your foot, whistling, giggling, or throwing papers, stop doing it. Your teacher can and will lower your grade if you continually disturb the class and provoke her—whether or not it's fair. Teachers do it all the time. It's the only real power they have to control your actions, so they use it, and there's nothing much you can do about it.

Not fair, you say, I should be marked on my work and not on my behavior. "Should." A very nice word. But that's not the way it works. Many teachers will find a way to legitimately lower your grade if you drive them up the wall, even if they have to count your classwork (that is, your bad behavior) as a major part of your grade.

It's time to face the fact that when someone has authority over you, it's wise to comply with that person's wishes, at least insofar as they relate to minor things such as gum chewing and giggling. You won't always be the one who has to do the compromising. The day will come when you will be in a position to demand that others alter their behavior to suit you. Whether you're a parent, a manager, or a boss, you will some day have power over someone else's life. At that time you can search your conscience and decide how fair you want to be, remembering your own feelings of what it was like not to have such power. Until then, accept the reality of the situation and go along with your teacher's requests, even if they seem unreasonable—so long as they don't violate your conscience.

–SHE TAKES HER BAD MOOD OUT ON US*#*#*#–

When my teacher is in a bad mood, everyone knows it. She comes in and starts screaming at the class for any little thing—at the top of her lungs. On another day, we could have done the same thing and she wouldn't have said a word.

Sandra, 17

Of course it isn't fair that a teacher come to class in a bad mood and take it out on her students. Similarly, it isn't fair when your parents come home from a bad day at the office and take it out on you; and it isn't fair that just because you had a fight with your best friend, you snap at your little brother. But people are human, and at times they will be less than perfect, so let's stop demanding perfection. When you come to think of it, since it is impossible to be perfect, expecting perfection of your teacher is, in itself, unfair.

–WHY CAN'T WE PICK OUR OWN SEATS?–

Why do we have to sit where the teacher tells us to sit? You would think we were in first grade or something!!

Karen, 16

My teacher asked me to sit in the back of the room, and then when I said no, she started saying stuff in Spanish. I didn't know what she was saying, but it sounded like she was cursing me out, so I got mad and told her to shut up. Then she wrote a blue card on me.

Sherman, 16

Karen hates assigned seats. So did I because I'm short, and since my last name then was Yellin, I always ended up in the back row. I didn't just leave it at that, however. I usually asked to sit in the front so I could see, and my request was usually granted.

The truth is, most teachers are quite fair, and if you have a good reason for a seat change, they will probably grant it. If, however, your goal is to sit next to a friend so that the two of you can talk and disturb the class, you better believe that the teacher is going to be fair *to himself* and say no. He's going to seat you exactly where you will be the least problem to him—and why shouldn't he?

Teachers are trying to survive, and they have a right to decide where each student sits. If Sherman had moved willingly, he wouldn't have provoked the teacher and the whole unpleasant episode, culminating in a blue card, would never have occurred. It doesn't pay to waste your energy on these no-win situations.

–BUT I DIDN'T DO IT–

Someone threw a paper that hit the teacher, and she blamed me. We got into an argument and I ended up in the principal's office. That was not fair because I couldn't tell that my friend did it, so it made me look guilty. Nobody believed me.

Joey, 13

Joey's situation is frustrating. Most people become very upset when falsely accused, especially if they can't, for whatever reason, prove their innocence. Joey's difficult choice was to expose his friend or take the blame.

In life, many times you will be given unfair choices. All you can do is evaluate your options and choose the lesser of two evils. If the price of silence is no more than a scolding, perhaps it is worth more to Joey to remain loyal to his friend. If the price is higher—suspension from school, or a bad mark on a report card—then he may not be willing to keep quiet. Only Joey can decide how high a price he's willing to pay to protect his friend.

-SURPRISE QUIZ-

Why does the teacher have to punish the whole class just because one person does something wrong? A few people were making noise in the back and wouldn't quiet down so the teacher got mad and made all of us take a quiz on the work. Now you know that's not fair.

Samantha, 14

It's not fair to give the whole class a quiz because of a few students, but teachers do it—myself included. Why? Because it's the best way I know of getting instant quiet and regaining control of the class when students are making too much noise for me to be able to teach. It also allows me to kill three other birds with one stone: I give myself a chance to cool off; I teach the class a lesson—that if they don't heed my warnings to be quiet in the future, a quiz is coming; and I find out which students have been doing their work!!!

Teachers often do things in anger that may not be completely fair but do serve a legitimate end—keeping control of the class. Without that control, no learning can take place. And that would be even more unfair to those who aren't causing the trouble than having to take a surprise quiz. Besides, it's the teacher's job to find out if you are keeping up with the work. If she's smart enough to kill more than one bird with a stone, good for her. You'll be the ultimate beneficiary of that wisdom.

–BUT I HAVE TO GO TO THE BATHROOM–

When you have to go to the bathroom, you have to go. There ought to be a law that says a teacher can't stop you from going to relieve yourself. It's so unfair that you have to sit there and squirm just because too many other people asked to be excused. And the worst part is, you get the same story in each class, and if you go between periods, you're late for class and you get in trouble.

Britt, 16

Britt has a legitimate complaint. If I had my way, students would be allowed to get up and go to the lavatory with no pass, and simply slip quietly back into their seats when they returned. In fact, I tried it in one class, and for the most part, it worked very well. Unfortunately, a few students ruined it for the rest—you know, the ones who left not to use the lavatory, but to spend twenty minutes in the hall talking to their friends—so I had to discontinue the experiment. Because of similar experiences, most teachers are suspicious of those who ask for the bathroom pass, and tend to be very stingy with it.

If you are frustrated by this problem and find that it's causing you genuine discomfort in your classes, the matter can be very simply resolved. Ask your parent to write a note to the effect that you have a bladder problem and need to be excused for the bathroom for a quick five minutes when you ask. No teacher would deny such a request once he had verified that the note was actually written by your parent.

–WHO EVER SAID LIFE IS FAIR?–

The word fair means "equal" or "just." When something is not fair, it's not equal to what you deserve. It often works out in life that you don't get exactly what you deserve. Why? Because, unfortunately, life is not fair.

Fairness is an ideal, something we strive for, but it certainly isn't anything that is guaranteed in the *Bill of Rights* or even in the Bible. In fact, even in those precious documents, fairness is advocated as an ideal—a goal to strive for in our treatment of others. By definition, however, the ideal differs from reality.

Sometimes, of course, we're happy that life isn't fair. When you get a lucky break—one that you don't necessarily deserve, such as finding money on the street, or getting a good grade just because your teacher likes you, or getting to go out with the hottest person in the school— aren't you glad? If you won the lottery, even though you only played it once while someone else played it a thousand times and never won, would you complain? Of course not.

The fact is, if life were perfectly "fair" at every moment in time, we would be bored to death. All of the challenge and adventure would be gone. Given the reality that life throws lots of curves our way, what we have to do is learn to make the most of every opportunity. Sometimes we can even hit a home run off one of those curve balls. So don't spend your time complaining about the unfairness of it all. Come out swinging, and you may turn your bad luck into good.

–BUT I DESERVE AN 85!!!–

Students often complain about unfair marks, and teachers generally have answers for them—but not answers students like to hear.

I busted my chops doing homework, papers, tests, and classwork. I thought I should have gotten at least an 85, or more. So I asked Mr. Hill why he gave me a 70, and he said, "Be happy that you got that."

Ted, 16

What should Ted have done in such a situation? Teachers say:

We make mistakes, too. If a student feels cheated about his mark, he should ask to go over the tests, classroom participation, and homework marks. I do that, and if I find that I've made an error, I change the mark.

English teacher, 16 years

I explained to one angry student that while he did get 80s and 90s during the last marking period, he got 50s and 60s for his first two marking periods, so his final grade should be 75. He understood, but still thought I should give more weight to the last marking period. To me, *that* wouldn't be fair to those who worked hard for the entire semester.

Biology teacher, 10 years

You just can't please some kids. I explain to them that I'm the teacher, and in the end, I have to make a judgment. However, I'm always willing to carefully review the records.

Economics teacher, 17 years

The answer is clear. In a respectful voice, you should ask the teacher to go over the records with you. (There's no sense in putting the teacher on the defensive.) Your teacher may or may not be correct, but until you see it in black and white, you're going to feel cheated.

Most likely, the teacher will agree to this review, but if not, you could speak to the department chairperson. Since every student has a right to know how his or her mark was determined, no chairperson would deny such a request.

–HE NEVER GIVES BACK THE TESTS–

I hate to bother taking tests in that class. You know you're never going to see them until two months later. By then, who cares?

Jeremy, 13

It is most annoying when teachers take forever to return a test, and it is unfair to the students, because it doesn't give them the kind of feedback they need to understand their mistakes and correct them for the future. If your teacher does this, you have the right to start nagging after a couple of weeks have gone by, and you could tell the rest of the class to do the same. Teachers know they should return tests within a week or two. Your constant reminders will help to re-awaken their sense of responsibility, which sometimes gets lazy or goes to sleep, just as yours does.

-*NOW* SHE CALLS ON ME!!!-

I could have my hand up for a year, and my teacher will never all on me. Then when my hand is not up, sure enough, he calls on me. It's just not fair.

Ursula, 14

Ursula's teacher is using the oldest teaching trick in the book. He calls on those who do not raise their hands in order to catch them if they are not paying attention. If your teacher does this to you, why not try a trick of your own: Stop raising your hand, and then when she calls on you, be ready with a brilliant answer.

If that doesn't work, all you have to do is speak to your teacher after class and ask her to call on you more often when your hand is up. We teachers do appreciate our "regulars," the ones who always have their hands up. Without you, we would be lost. But sometimes in our diligence to catch the sleepers, we take you for granted and neglect you. It's a good idea to remind us from time to time.

-SHE NEVER REVIEWS FOR A TEST-

When my teacher gives a test, she won't review or even give us a hint about what's on it. All she says is, "Study everything." That's ridiculous.

Ro, 15

Teachers who refuse to review for a test are hoping that their students will study everything. Technically speaking, that's just what students are supposed to do—know all of the material taught. Your teacher is under no obligation to review for the test. If she does review, lucky you. If she does not, it looks like you'll have to put your shoulder to the grindstone and study everything. If you do this, in the long run you will be better off than those who had teachers who spoon-fed them the test. You will have learned more. Isn't that what school is all about? Learning?

–HOMEWORK ON FRIDAYS–

It's not fair when teachers give homework on Fridays. Just because they're old and worn out and have nothing to do with their time but mark papers on the weekends, doesn't mean we have nothing better to do. We're young and we want to enjoy our youth. Someone should talk to these teachers.

Gwen, 15

Homework on Friday. I give it all the time. Why? Because you have two whole days instead of one night in which to do it. I'm also trying to prepare my students for the future. When you go out into the cruel world to "seek your fortune," you will quickly find out that work is not always a nine-to-five, Monday through Friday business, especially if you're ambitious. You discover that those two wonderful weekend days are golden opportunities to catch up on important work.

Having to do homework on the weekends also encourages you to learn how to budget your leisure time—to decide whether you want to get your work out of the way first and play later, or the reverse. In addition, you'll find out what kind of self-discipline you have. For example, if you know you have homework due on Monday, and you say to yourself, "I'll do it Sunday," but never get around to it, you'll have learned an important lesson about yourself. You will have discovered that for you, as for most of us, it's necessary to put business before pleasure. Learning this lesson during your school years and following through on it by making it a habit to work now and play later can save you a lifetime of trouble.

Maybe I'm prejudiced in favor of teachers because I am one, but I do think that even when they are being unfair, you can learn from the situation and put the lessons to use in later life. Most of the time, however, the actions students view as unfair—from assigning homework on weekends, to giving pop quizzes, to insisting on a standard of behavior that doesn't include gum chewing or foot stomping—are ultimately for their own benefit. If you seriously disagree, you can go to the authorities about your teacher's behavior and see to it that either the behavior is changed, or your class is changed. It's up to you to decide if the abuse is serious enough to warrant your taking such a step.

–REMINDERS–

1. Some teachers will have "pets" whether you like it or not. As long as your grade is not affected, live and let live.

2. If your teacher is picking on you, try to figure out whether it's a personality conflict that is causing the trouble, or something specific you're doing that gets on the teacher's nerves. If it's personality, perhaps you can speak to the teacher and turn things around. If not, so what. You can't win em all!! If it's something you're doing that has annoyed the teacher, simply stop it. Why make trouble for yourself.

3. If you resent adjusting your behavior to suit others, realize that all successful people do this to some extent. That's what it takes to get along with people.

4. It may not be fair, but most people take their moods out on those around them—at least once in a while. Don't you do it, too? So try to have a little patience with your teachers. Think what they put up with every day.

5. If you feel as if you were cheated on your grade, ask the teacher to go over the records with you. Every student has that right, and most teachers are more than willing to look things over again. If you don't ask, you'll never know.

6. Where is it written that in life, everyone is guaranteed a "fair shake"? Fairness is an ideal or a goal to which we should all aspire, both for ourselves and for others. But we also have to accept the reality that life is not always fair. Look around you. You'll probably see lots of examples of unfairness much worse than the ones you've suffered.

9

Chaotic, Confused, and Out of Control

They would throw spitballs when her back was turned. People would call out and walk around the room. One day she even cried in front of the class.

Pam, 14

We used to call this teacher names, like Mr. Potato Head and Kojak, because he was bald. Finally, one day he cursed at the whole class.

John, 16

In this chapter we'll talk about teachers who scream at the top of their lungs, throw things, and even curse. We'll talk about teachers who flirt with students, as well as those who go so far as to make sexual comments and advances. In other words, we'll discuss teachers who are chaotic, confused, or out of control—in that order.

–THE CHAOTIC CLASSROOM–

Everyone is yelling at the top of their lungs. The teacher just threw a book at a student. Erasers and chalk are flying through the air, occasionally hitting their mark—the teacher. The teacher is continually screaming over and over. "You're all getting failing grades." What's wrong with this picture? Why do some teachers lose control of their classes?

If you are in high school now, perhaps you can recall such scenes from junior high, where they are particularly likely to occur, because of the "growing pains" of students in their early teens. These are the "dreaded" years for many teachers, the years when students are most difficult to handle—the time when they are passing from childhood into teenhood and their hormones are "leaping." It takes an especially gifted teacher to deal effectively with people in this age group, who would often try the patience of a saint.

–NEW TEACHERS HAVE A DIFFICULT TIME–

I was a new teacher and I really didn't know what I was doing. The kids sensed this and took full advantage of me. After I got wise to the ways of teenagers things changed. It took about two years.

English teacher, 5 years

New teachers often have a hard time maintaining order in a class. Even though they are "supposed to" know how to control a class of teenagers, they don't always do well at it when they're just starting out. Teachers, like most people, learn from experience, and no amount of book-learning or student teaching can substitute for the first couple of years in one's own classroom. When you think of it, it's a wonder teachers have as much control as they do.

–OVERCROWDED CLASSES–

Sometimes they give me overcrowded classes. When this happens it's hard to learn anyone's name because there aren't enough seats, so no one ever sits in the same place twice, and it's like musical chairs. This happened to me last year. When students acted up, I couldn't even mark them down, because I wasn't sure of their names—and when I asked, they would never tell me the right one.

French teacher, 7 years

The bigger the class, the more difficult it is to control—especially if you happen to get a bunch of "live wires" all in one class.

As unfair as it may be to teachers, they are often forced to teach classes with far too many students, at least until there's a redistribution that divides them more equally among all the teachers. When this happens, it can prove impossible to maintain discipline in the crucial first few weeks of the term. And once the pattern has been set, it's often difficult to regain control, even after the classes have been equalized.

–SPEAKING OF "LIVE WIRES"–

Last semester, as luck would have it, I got every "class clown" in the school. I couldn't keep them quiet or in their seats no matter what I did. Finally I started calling their homes. That helped a little, but to tell the truth, I was thinking of retiring. Now, thank God, I have a group of calm, respectful young adults. I love them.

Social studies teacher, 22 years

Sometimes what happens in class is just sheer luck—all of it bad. A teacher will occasionally get more than his share of mischief makers in a class. When this happens, especially to an inexperienced teacher, the personalities of these rambunctious individuals interact and *voilà*—you have a constant eruption of some sort. This is "class chemistry" at its worst.

In some schools, a teacher can appeal to the chairperson and ask to have a few instigators removed. However, this may not always be possible. Maybe all the other teachers already have their own share of troublemakers. If this is the case, the teacher may experiment with various methods of control—giving demerits, calling homes, keeping the class very busy at all times, or using compliments and rewards. Sometimes they work, sometimes not. But the truth is, most teachers would feel the way the twenty-two-year veteran of social studies did—tempted to retire. Some years are so awful that you can only thank God when the term ends and hope for better luck next term.

–TOO MANY EMOTIONALLY DISTURBED STUDENTS–

Some teenagers need psychiatric help. They really shouldn't be in a regular classroom. But they are, so when you get enough of these in a class, all you can do is try to make it to the bell.

Remedial reading teacher, 17 years

Sometimes a teacher is given more than a few emotionally disturbed students, and that number is enough to throw what would otherwise be a calm, controlled class into a frenzy. Teachers are not usually given many psychology courses during their training, and they don't always know how to handle neurotic or high-strung teenagers. Yet today, as the divorce rate increases and with drug-and alcohol-related problems on the rise, not to mention the added tensions of everyday life in this increasingly complicated world, there are more and more young adults in need of professional help—teenagers who are incapable of sitting in a classroom all day long without becoming a problem to the teacher and those around them.

–IT TAKES A SPECIAL TALENT–

Some teachers who may be very intelligent and highly educated simply have no real ability in group management—especially teen group management. So why did they become teachers, you may ask. Perhaps because they didn't find out in time to change their field. Student teaching in and of itself is not enough to tell the tale, because it isn't "the real thing." Most classes regularly give these novices a hard time, and student teachers are always told, "Don't worry. You'll get the hang of it, once you start teaching." Fortunately, in time, most of us do. But some teachers you may encounter never do catch on, because they lack the basic talent for handling teenagers. These are often the people who keep plugging away, hoping things will eventually improve if they wait long enough. They have already committed themselves to a career in teaching—having spent up to six years in college preparing for their career.

Of course, it's never too late (though it may be very expensive) to admit a mistake, and luckily, many unhappy teachers do. Once they realize that teaching is not suited to their talents, they take the necessary steps and move on to another career. But others stubbornly remain where they are. Perhaps they don't feel like starting over. They dread going back to school or searching for a job in an unrelated field. Or they think they'll eventually get the hang of it. So they "stick it out," enduring an unhappy existence in a profession they should have left years ago—unless by good luck (which may not seem like it at the time) they are asked to leave.

–THE FORGETFUL TEACHER–

Teachers sometimes forget things—important things, like your name, or the homework they assign. Students can get very upset when they feel no one is paying attention to them or their work.

> Even after two months, my English teacher still doesn't know my name. That's depressing.
>
> *Tanya, 15*

> The reason I don't do homework is that when I spent hours doing it, he always forgot to check it. What's the use of doing homework if he's not even going to look at it?
>
> *Danny, 14*

Some people are better at remembering names than others, but even some memory experts would have a difficult time memorizing 150 names in a matter of weeks. What amazes me is not how many teachers *don't* remember their students' names, but how many *do*—and what's more, how many remember them when they meet by chance years later.

If your teacher doesn't remember your name, you may

think he does not remember *you*; but that may not be the case at all. Speaking for myself, even if I forget a name, I often feel that I know the person very well. I know that student's personality, whether he's quiet or gentle; deep or intense; light-hearted or bubbly. I know what my students wear, who their parents are, what grades they make, where they live, and often, even what makes them happiest and saddest; and still, I sometimes just draw a blank when I try to remember their names.

Other times I'll meet a student and not feel that his or her name matches my sense of who he is. For example, I may have a student named Gary, but every time I look at him, I think "Anthony." To me, he's an Anthony, and no matter what he says, I can't help but think "Anthony." He may feel offended, assuming I don't care enough about him to remember his name; but the opposite is true. I've got such a vivid sense of who he is that I've renamed him in my own mind to suit my image of him.

Of course, sometimes it's not just names that we teachers forget; sometimes it's the work that we assign. We are usually overloaded with work and cut corners where we can. One of the corners that can end up getting cut is checking homework. Danny's problem with the teacher who never looks at homework can be easily solved, however. He can speak to the teacher after class and tell him how he feels: "When you don't check homework, it makes me feel as if I'm wasting my time, because I never find out if I did it right. Can't you check mine every day?" Most teachers would respond to such a request and check at least that student's homework even if they continued to neglect the rest. Why? Teachers know they're supposed to check homework, and when reminded, they'll do it if only to keep themselves out of trouble.

If every student asked to be checked, surely the teacher would comply. But this will never happen, and you know why? I've never, in the history of my twenty-five years of teaching, seen an entire class do their homework. Have you?

–TEACHERS WHO CURSE AT AND INSULT THEIR STUDENTS–

Why do some teachers descend to the level of their worst students? Is it inevitable that if you teach long enough you become just like a teenager? Of course not. But there are things that might drive a teacher—or anyone—to swearing. Here's one student's account.

> We would throw stink bombs in his room and put books over the door and let them drop on his head. One day he was chasing this kid, and he ran straight into a cabinet—man, you should have heard him curse!!!
>
> *Allen, 14*

I surveyed many teachers to see if they ever cursed at their students, and if so, why. Surprisingly, there were quite a few who admitted to having done so. Here's what they said:

> It's not right, but I just lose it sometimes when they get me to a certain point.
>
> *Social studies teacher, 19 years*

> The closest I ever came was when I cursed under my breath and this student heard me. No one had done the homework for the third time that week, and I was very frustrated.
>
> *Science teacher, 17 years*

One time I called a girl an a------. She was really getting sarcastic with me, and it just popped out of my mouth. She reported me to the principal, and I was very embarrassed.

English teacher, 26 years

–"TELL IT TO YOUR MOTHER," SAID DR. JONES–

I have been teaching for twenty-five years, and during those years I have had the opportunity to see even the most composed, cultured people lose control. I shall never forget the time, early one winter morning, just before the first period was about to begin, when I stepped onto the elevator and encountered Dr. Jones, a highly intellectual science teacher with a distinguished-sounding British accent. He and a student who had just gotten off the elevator were having an argument, and when the student hurled an insult at him, this dignified gentleman replied, as the elevator doors drew shut and the student's mouth fell open, "Tell it to your mother." All the teachers in the elevator burst out laughing.

If the students could drive even Dr. Jones to such a point, is there hope for any of us?

Of course it is not right for teachers to say such things or to curse, and the majority of us do not. But all of us do, on occasion, lose our tempers; and when we do, we can erupt into some most unprofessional outbursts.

-SHOULD YOU REPORT US?-

Do teenagers like it when teachers curse in front of the class? Not at all. If your teacher uses foul language or insults you, evaluate the situation. If it's a rare occurrence, and in response to extreme provocation, as was the case with Dr. Jones, you should probably laugh it off and forgive it. But if it happens all the time, and it upsets you, you really shouldn't have to put up with it. Consider making a complaint to the department chairperson. And don't worry. The teacher isn't going to be fired on the spot. The chairperson will talk to the teacher, giving him or her a chance to correct the situation. If, however, the teacher continues to curse, insult, or otherwise misbehave, and if enough students report it, you can be sure that something will eventually be done. That teacher will not be there for long.

-SHE SHOULDN'T DRESS THAT WAY!!-

My teacher wears tight short skirts, and all the boys sit in the first row so they can get a look. I think it's disgusting. That teacher even flirts with people's boyfriends.

Cheryl, 15

Why do teachers sometimes dress in a seductive manner? For many reasons. Some teachers need the attention that a sexy skirt or an ultra-tight pair of jeans will get them. But others are unaware of the inappropriateness of their dress. They're genuinely thinking only of their preference in clothing, and they forget all about propriety. It never occurs to them that their dress could be offensive to anyone. In fact, they probably think they look gorgeous, and maybe they do—but they should save it for a night-club, not the classroom. They need to be reminded that there's a time and place to be seductive, and that school is neither.

Why doesn't someone in authority tell such a teacher to correct her dress? In many schools she would be reprimanded by her chairperson or principal—that is, if either one of them happened to notice. In other schools no one cares, perhaps because there are too many other things to worry about.

If your teacher's dress bothers you a lot, why not ask your parent to write a note to the chairperson? The chairperson will probably speak to the teacher discreetly, and the wise teacher will modify her dress. If the teacher continues to dress in an unsuitable fashion, the next step is to speak to the principal. Not too many teachers would ignore the situation then.

–OTHER INAPPROPRIATE DRESS–

He had long dirty hair, and he wore a headband and beads and faded jeans. You would think he just stepped out of the sixties.

Jennifer, 17

My teacher wears shorts in the summer and talks just like we do. He uses all our expressions, trying to be cool, but he sounds stupid. Why doesn't he act his age?

Tommy, 15

Jennifer's teacher was probably a teenager in the sixties, and he wants to remain a teenager—so he continues to dress the way the young adults of his day dressed. Is he harming anyone by his out-of-style dress? I doubt it. In my opinion, as long as he's teaching the lesson and his students are learning what they're supposed to be learning, dress shouldn't be an issue.

The same goes for Tommy's teacher. He wears bermuda shorts and uses the same expressions as the kids. Evidently he too wishes to remain a teenager, but Tommy didn't criticize his teaching, only his dress. If you have such a teacher, but he's doing his job properly, chances are you'll do what Tommy does—think to yourself, "Why doesn't he act his age?" and leave it at that. There's really no harm done, even if you do think he looks ridiculous.

–TEACHERS SHOULDN'T DATE STUDENTS—EVER–

My math teacher is very young, and he's dating this girl who is a senior. Everybody knows about it, but no one does anything. Can teachers do that? I don't think it's right.

Joe, 17

Teachers should never date students, and in most school systems such behavior would be grounds for dismissal. To date a student is to take advantage of a vulnerable young person. Teachers should be expected to use enough self-control to avoid that situation, even if it is tempting, and even if the age difference is not that great. For example, a twenty-three-year-old teacher may be very attracted to an eighteen-year-old student. What can he do? He can wait until she graduates and then ask her out. There's more at issue than the five years that separate them. There is a gulf of power and status that distinguishes teachers from students and puts the students at a great disadvantage in romantic, and/or sexual situations. Once the eighteen-year-old is no longer a student at the teacher's school, that gulf can be bridged, which will help to equalize the relationship.

-YOU MUST REPORT
SEXUAL OFFENSES-

We had this teacher who would make sexual comments about everything. It was disgusting. We reported him many times, and finally he left. I heard he got fired.

Jody, 14

One time my art teacher, brushed against me in the wrong place. I know he did it on purpose because I've seen him pat girls on their behind and laugh as if it was a joke. I told my mother, and she said if it ever happens again she's reporting it to the principal.

Juliet, 15

Teachers who make sexual comments and advances to students must be stopped immediately. There is no excuse for such behavior and, if reported, such teachers would be quickly stopped or, if the complaints continued, fired. But the only way to make sure that action is taken is to make a complaint, no matter how unpleasant that may be. I don't think Juliet's mother should wait to see if another such incident occurs with her daughter. I think she should report the teacher *NOW*.

-TEACHERS, LIKE ANYONE ELSE, CAN GO ASTRAY-

It's easy to forget that teachers are human beings. Like anyone else, they can give way to sexual temptation, take drugs, become alcoholics, and worse. So it's certainly not surprising that teachers can lose control of classes, become extremely forgetful, snap and curse at the class, behave or dress in an immature fashion, and in other ways not live up to the standards of the profession.

If your teacher demonstrates any of the behaviors mentioned in this chapter, it's up to you to decide whether or not the situation merits action. If it does, by all means, don't wait for someone else to take the first step. Everyone else is probably waiting, too. That's why these things go on for as long as they sometimes do. Take action *now*.

On the other hand, you may decide that the offense the teacher is committing is so minor that it can be overlooked. If that is the case, go on with your life. In time, that teacher will be just a memory, and probably a funny one at that.

-REMINDERS-

1. If your teacher can't control the class, it may be because: the teacher is new, the class is overcrowded, there are too many emotionally disturbed students in the class, or, as luck would have it, the "class chemistry" just works that way.

2. Teachers admit to having cursed at classes when provoked beyond the breaking point. Though the circumstances don't justify such a loss of control, they

may explain it. It's probably not worth reporting unless it happens repeatedly.

3. If your teacher dresses, behaves, or talks like a teenager, chances are he's trying in vain to remain a teenager. Learn from his mistake and make sure you don't fall into the same trap when you become an adult. But don't bother to report him. He's harmless, even if he looks silly to you.

4. Teachers who dress or talk in a sexually provocative way need to be reminded of the proprieties by their chairperson, parents, or principal.

5. Teachers who date students, or who make sexual comments or advances, should not be tolerated. The reason teacher-student abuse sometimes goes on for extended periods of time is that most teenagers tend not to report it. Don't wait for someone else to take action. Report any student-teacher sexual activity immediately.

10

Burned Out!!!

All he did was sit there and read the paper while we wrote essays or read the book.

Joanne, 16

Cynical, burned-out teachers are the worst. They give the students low morale.

Tricia 14

Teachers who don't care about their job shouldn't be teaching. What do they have to offer?

Rich, 15

Everyone has heard the expression "burnout," but what does it really mean? When it comes to teachers, burnouts are people who have lost their enthusiasm for teaching. They no longer feel the fire of inspiration that called them to the profession in the first place. Worn out, both physically and mentally, they trudge to work every day, recalling only vaguely a time when they couldn't wait to get back from summer vacation because they missed the students so much.

In this chapter we'll find out why teachers get burned out, and how some teachers have overcome burnout. But more importantly, we'll talk about how you can have a positive effect on a burned-out teacher—and maybe even rekindle the flame of inspiration in him or her. Even if you don't care about the teacher's well-being, you may want to do something to keep from dying of boredom in his class.

-THE WELL RUNS DRY-

Teachers get burned out for many reasons, some that are easily handled and others that are more difficult. But no matter how bad the burnout, there's always a way for you to make the best of the situation. First, let's try to understand the problem. Then we'll talk about solutions.

Teachers give and give and give. On a daily basis, they pour their hearts and souls out to the students—and the better the teacher, the more they pour out. After ten, fifteen, or even twenty years of this giving, it is inevitable that a teacher feel drained.

After a while, teachers become physically as well as emotionally exhausted. It takes an awful lot of energy to keep up with over 150 teenagers day after day. Although being around teens keeps teachers young in many ways, in other ways it can make them feel very old. Plain and simple, teachers need a rest. They need a break from the general noise and energy level of being in a school filled with excited, mischievous teenagers. And they need the intellectual stimulation of a fresh look at their own discipline. To meet these needs, teachers may go on sabbatical, an opportunity to take time off from teaching (with about two-thirds pay) every seven years so that they can travel, go back to college, rest and relax, or just have some fun— whatever it takes to become rejuvinated and eager to teach again.

-THE POWER OF
THE SABBATICAL-

Although in many school systems a teacher is allowed a sabbatical every seven years, many teachers do not avail themselves of it. Why?

Some teachers don't take advantage of the sabbatical because they can't afford the cut in pay. Since teachers are not highly paid and are not allowed to take other paying work during their sabbaticals, many have to refuse the opportunity.

Some teachers feel that taking time off is equivalent to admitting defeat. Although they feel exhausted and drained, rather than admit to human weakness, they forge ahead, trying to tough it out in the hope that the feeling will pass. When it doesn't, their burnout deepens into depression. Only then do some of them give in and take a sabbatical—if they haven't pushed themselves so far that they have to retire from teaching completely.

Perhaps it was a teacher who had waited too long who added a line to the following saying, which was hung on the wall of the English department in a New York City high school:

> The mediocre teacher tells
> The good teacher explains
> The superior teacher demonstrates
> The great teacher inspires

And then the penciled-in line:

> The smart teacher retires!!!

Another reason teachers don't always take advantage of the sabbatical is fear of change. Many teachers have been in school practically all of their lives—at least since they were about five years old. Can you imagine how difficult it must be for them to even contemplate the thought of not getting up and "going to school" every morning? "What would I do?" they wonder. "I'll be bored to death," they fear. "If I get out of the habit of my routine, I may not be able to return to it," they worry. So they carry on, becoming more and more burned out each day.

Too bad these teachers don't overcome their doubts and take advantage of this much-needed opportunity to get away from teaching. If they did, they might find that the sabbatical works wonders. As the following teachers indicate, some return to teaching with an entirely new attitude:

> Teaching became extremely trying. I felt exhausted all the time. I didn't have it in me to get excited about the lesson. Finally I took a sabbatical and now I'm all fired up again.
>
> *English teacher, 23 years*

> Every morning I would dread walking into that building. I would waste half the period on the "Do Now." I knew I was cheating the kids so I took a six-month sabbatical. When I came back, to my surprise, the rest had revived me. I was excited again. I had more patience. Who would think time off could do all that?
>
> *Biology teacher, 20 years*

> I wondered if I were doing any good—if I should be doing something else. I took a leave of absence, not a sabbatical, because with a sabbatical, you're not allowed to work at another job—just rest, study, or travel. I worked in the business world for a year. I hated it. I missed the kids. It was then that I realized how important it was to me to be a positive influence

on someone. Now I love teaching. I wouldn't trade it for the world.

English teacher, 11 years

–I THOUGHT I COULD CHANGE THE WORLD— WHAT HAPPENED?–

Teachers often become burned out because they temporarily lose faith in their profession. Chances are, they enter teaching with high hopes of changing the world by making a major impact on its youth. Then, once they enter the system, they have to deal with administrations that tie their hands and do not allow them to function as professionals. Bogged down with paperwork, and subject to all kinds of pressures, they become discouraged. This is a stage in almost every teacher's life. Each of us has had to figure out a way to be a good teacher *in spite of* the administration and to accept the fact that we may only be able to change a few lives and not the world.

–TEACHERS NEED INSPIRATION–

"I get the same pay, whether you learn this or not."

I'll bet a teacher has said this to your class once or twice. If so, she probably said it in a moment of frustration when the class wasn't paying attention and she was pouring her heart out trying to explain some important point.

Teachers are frustrated on a daily basis. You can see them every day darting around the front of the room, enthusiastically demonstrating some theory, idea, or profound truth while the faces of their "congregation" remain blank. How do they do it? What keeps them going? When you come to think about it, it's no wonder that some teachers burn out. It's a wonder that some don't.

Teachers become defensive when they are continually given the cold, indifferent stare that so often greets them as they do their dance in front of the room—dancing, as it were, without a partner. "Maybe I should just think of this as a job and stop worrying about whether it makes a difference in anyone's life," they think.

The problem is, it's very hard for teachers to convince themselves not to care. If they didn't care, they wouldn't have chosen this profession. Eventually, however, if they never get any positive feedback from their students, they retreat into a shell. They stop pouring their hearts out, and they put in only the minimum effort—giving busy work to the class while they wait for the bell to ring. This makes them even more miserable. They feel guilty, frustrated, and useless. The less they do, the worse they feel. They hate their jobs, and they hate their lives, and they feel powerless to change the situation.

–HOW TO SAVE YOUR TEACHER FROM BURNING OUT–

Not so long ago I was really depressed about teaching. "I'm wasting my time," I thought. "It's like talking to the wall," I grumbled. "I've spent my youth in this place," I moaned, "and for what?" Then I went to my mailbox and found a letter. It was from Frank Kovak, a former student of mine. I remembered him right away. He used to sit in the back of the room, appearing to pay little attention to the lesson while I did everything in my power to win him over and get him involved. Though he did come to class every day and managed to pass the course with a mediocre grade, he never gave me any indication that I was getting through to him, no matter how hard I tried. For this reason, I was very surprised when I read the letter, which said that he would never forget me because I was one of the few teachers who had tried to reach out to him. He thanked me for taking the time to tell him that he had talent, and encouraging him to believe that he was born for a reason, one that he would find if he went in search of it.

He told me that after joining the army, fresh out of school, he had decided to pursue a career in the military, and that he was about to be promoted to a very high position. The letter ended with his telling me that he wished there were more people like me in the world.

If only someone could have recorded my thoughts and actions during the five minutes it took me to open that letter and read it as I walked down the street toward the restaurant where I usually eat lunch. I would imagine that my face and my bearing changed as dramatically as my mood. Suddenly I wasn't tired. I felt tears of joy well up in my eyes. I thought: "If Frank, who never even seemed to be listening, felt this way, who knows how many other thousands of teenagers I may have helped over the years." (By now I've taught over seven thousand.) And then I had the strength to go on.

I'm not alone. Other discouraged teachers have felt the same lift in response to something a student has said. Sometimes the smallest crumb of encouragement can make it all seem worthwhile. Listen to some of my colleagues talk about the moments that have given them hope.

My last class was a group of potential dropouts who were having attendance problems. Whenever anyone was absent, I would make a big deal out of how much I missed that person. My method really reached home with one boy, because not only did he end up with a nearly perfect attendance record, he got a 97 on the chemistry regents. He told me that I was the first teacher he met who even noticed that he was alive. It made me think of what a long way a little love can go, and how important the role of teacher really is.

Science teacher, 15 years

A girl who was reading on third-grade level when she came into my class graduated with a reading score of 12.6. On graduation day she came up to me and said, "You were the only one who believed in me." All the money in the world cannot buy the feeling you have when something like that happens.

Language arts teacher, 14 years

A very shy boy who spoke to no one gave me the greatest compliment of my life. He said that if it weren't for me, he would still be thinking he was stupid. I remember how each time he would make a mistake he would call himself names, and I would say, "That's a common mistake. Even the smartest people make that mistake. Let's find out where we went off track." By the way, he's now an engineer.

Math teacher, 21 years

Without the inspiration of their students, teachers would have no motivation to go on. How sad it is that students rarely take the time to let a teacher know that he or she is doing some good.

-HAVE YOU SAID SOMETHING NICE TO YOUR TEACHER TODAY?-

Teachers are inspired and renewed by any evidence that their hard work has made a difference in someone's life. How often have you thought to yourself that a teacher had been helpful to you, in even a minor way, but never bothered to mention it to the teacher? Your comments mean a lot to us.

> "That was a good lesson."
>
> "You make the subject easy to understand."
>
> "You were really funny today."
>
> "I'm never bored in this class."
>
> "I thought about what you said. It helped me not to be so depressed."
>
> "I was tempted to neglect my homework until I remembered your words."
>
> "I can tell you really care about us. Teaching is not just a job to you, is it?"
>
> "Where do you get the energy to put up with us day after day? We give you such a hard time."
>
> "I'm so glad I had you for a teacher this term."

If you stop to think about it, you'll realize you have dozens of positive thoughts about your teachers each day, but most just pass through your mind without ever really registering. Why not catch one or two of them and pass them on? Don't use the samples I've mentioned above. Your own words will be better than mine, because they will come from your heart.

Next time, instead of just vaguely thinking a good thought about your teacher and letting it go, study your teacher and find something positive to say, something that is true. And then say it. I dare you.

"Nah, it's going to sound stupid," you say; or, "I'll look like I'm kissing up to the teacher"; or, "The teacher couldn't care less about what I think anyway." But trust me: Compliments never sound stupid to the receiver. They are the sweetest words in the English language. You won't look like you're trying to gain favor. You'll look like a mature young person who is not afraid to express himself. And, as I already mentioned, the teacher certainly does care about what you think. In fact, a good deal of your teacher's life revolves around what you think. So say it.

If you can't bring yourself to say something outright, why not write a note and slip it into the teacher's mailbox in the general office. You can ask that she not mention it to the class because you don't want the attention, and she will fully understand. But believe me, she'll be thrilled when she reads the note.

–IF YOU INSPIRE YOUR TEACHER, YOU'RE BOUND TO DO BETTER IN THAT CLASS–

Although you cannot force your burned-out teacher to take a sabbatical, you can do something to inspire him or her and change a dull, dreary class into an exciting one. How? Use the methods suggested in this book: Ask lots of questions in class, show a genuine interest in the subject, ask the teacher to give you special help if you need it, and compliment the teacher whenever you have an opportunity. The result will be that your teacher will gain a special appreciation for you and will go out of the way to help you to understand the material. Your mark will certainly be higher if you do this than if you sit in the back of the room thinking, "Man, this teacher is a burnout." Think about it. Am I right or wrong?

–REMINDERS–

1. Teachers become "burned out" for many reasons: They are physically and mentally exhausted, they have poured themselves out in an idealistic effort to change the world and have not seen the results they had hoped to see, and they suffer from lack of encouragement.

2. Teacher burnout is not fatal. There are several remedies: an extended vacation (sabbatical), a temporary change of job, or a little feedback from you—the student. Many "burned-out" teachers recover and go on to become even more inspired than before.

3. Teachers who recover from burnout say that they come back to teaching because they treasure the opportunity to make a difference where it counts—in the minds of their students.

4. Very few teachers remain in the profession indefinitely if they continue to feel burned out. They either take a sabbatical, retire, or move on to other careers.

5. You can make a major difference in the way your teacher feels about teaching. If you take the time to tell your teacher what he or she did to help you, what you liked about the lesson, or how you enjoyed his or her

sense of humor, your teacher will be inspired to go on teaching.

6. Teachers remember forever when a student takes the time to say, "You really made a difference."

11

The Wonderful Teacher

Most people have a favorite teacher in their past—a teacher they will never forget. If you question them about why that teacher was so special, the answer is usually the same: We learned so much besides the subject matter of the course. What was really being taught was self-confidence, self-discipline, and, most important, self-love—although we thought we were learning history (or English or math or whatever).

A good teacher doesn't just stand up in front of the class and lecture to you, but explains things clearly, so that you can understand, demonstrating where necessary with appropriate examples. A wonderful teacher goes a step further. That teacher inspires you to use your potential to the fullest, to believe in yourself and to achieve your goal in life. The wonderful teacher takes a personal interest in you.

Wonderful teachers have a message for students that goes beyond the limits of the subject matter, and they continually "preach" this message between the lines, as it were, even though they are not getting a dollar extra in their paycheck for doing so. They actually like their students—even love them—and they care about them to the point where they forget that teaching is only a job. In fact, they see teaching as an opportunity as well as a responsibility, allowing them to have a permanent influence on the lives of each and every one of their students.

Wonderful teachers also share another quality—a sense of humor. They take themselves and their students seriously, but not so seriously that they forget how to lighten up a bit.

-DO YOU HAVE A TEACHER YOU WILL NEVER FORGET?-

Think. Is there a teacher who went the extra mile for you, one who inspired you to reach for the best in yourself? Chances are, you can think of more than one teacher who did this. Teenagers talking about special teachers say:

> He showed me that I should be proud of myself even if I failed, as long as I gave it my best shot. He taught me how to pick myself up, brush myself off, and start all over again. Now, whenever I mess up or make a blunder, I don't quit. I start again. He was more like a mother and father all rolled into one—and not just a teacher.
>
> *Candy, 17*

> I was confused and upset about a boy who I wanted to break up with and who wouldn't leave me alone. I asked her what to do because she seemed like an understanding person. Her wise advice helped me to get out of a very sticky situation. I'll always thank her for not saying, "I'm busy right now."
>
> *Dana, 14*

I will never forget my English teacher. She told me she was fascinated by my creativity and placed me in honors even though my grades were not quite honors grades. Because she took a personal interest in me, I graduated in the top ten percent of my high school class. If it weren't for her, I doubt if I would even have gone to college.

Tricia, 19

My French teacher told me to congratulate myself whenever I achieved something, and to stop putting myself down every time I made a mistake. She helped me to laugh at myself instead of condemning myself, and later on I remembered her words. She took a lot of pressure off my life. In a way, you could say she was a psychologist to me.

Tracy, 16

I was crying because I didn't make a special high school for dance, and he sat me down and said, "It's up to you, not the school. Some day I will see you up on stage." Those words gave me the motivation and confidence to keep striving for my dream. Finally I made it into the city-wide dance team. That man deserves to be rewarded. I hope he wins the lottery or something because I know I'm not the only one he helped.

Anne, 16

My math teacher is one in a million—always ready with a funny joke, a witty comment. He made learning fun, and he really knew how to keep the class awake. But more than that, he went out of his way for the struggling student—me, for example. Because of him, I not only remained in honors math, I did well. He made sure everyone knew the subject. He never made anyone feel stupid. Instead he encouraged us to stick with it. I love that man.

Marthe, 17

My favorite teacher was my eighth-grade English teacher. He really liked me. I could tell. In fact, he liked the whole class. He made us feel like a family and not just a class.

Rob, 18

I wouldn't want to leave this subject without first telling you about the teacher who most influenced my life. Her name is Mrs. Zansky. She was my ninth-grade English teacher. I admired her because she was very intelligent, and she also seemed to have read every book in the library. In addition, she was a walking dictionary. I remember sitting in her class and wishing that I could some day become an English teacher, but worrying that I was not smart enough although I loved to read and was very interested in vocabulary. One day I dared to express my dream to her, adding, "but I know I'm not smart enough." I Half expect her to say, "You're right." I waited in dread for her to speak. Imagine my relief and surprise when she looked me straight in the eye and said: "I've always thought you would be a great English teacher, because you're not only very intelligent but extremely creative. In fact, you could be a writer, too."

I took her words to heart and turned them into a self-fulfilling prophecy. To this day, in my thoughts and in my heart I thank Mrs. Zansky for not crushing my dream, but for instead expressing belief in my ability to achieve my goal.

There are thousands of Mrs. Zanskys out there. I'm sure you could think of at least one yourself, and if you ask your parents, I'll bet they can think of one, too.

-TEACHERS HAVE
A "MESSAGE"-

Teachers who are really committed to their students—and that's most teachers—have a message for them over and above the subject matter of the course. What Rob and Marthe are telling us is that their teachers taught them some very important lessons—lessons not contained in the French, English, math, or history books. What are they? Obviously, they are inspirational lessons, lessons about how to believe in oneself and how to succeed in life.

I wondered if teachers realize that they do this sort of "preaching," so I decided to ask them as nonchalantly as possible: 'What is the 'message' or 'sermon' that you are trying to get across between the lines of your classroom lectures? Of course, I expected them to stop short and say something like, "What do you mean by sermon or message? I don't preach. This is not a church. I teach my subject and try to make sure my students learn it." But to my amazement, not one teacher challenged my question or even hesitated for a minute. In fact, each teacher gave an immediate response. Here are some of the answers I heard:

Use your potential—never settle for second best. Dare to go for your real goal. Don't look back and wonder about the "road not taken."

Be yourself. You're a unique individual, so don't yield to peer pressure. Do what's right for you.

Be honest and responsible. Treat people the way you wish to be treated. People respect those traits. If you have them, you will ultimately find yourself in a position of leadership.

Get as much as you can out of education. They can rob your house and steal your possessions, but no one can take away what you learn. Within your mind lies the potential to make a million dollars or change the world or do anything else. So learn, learn, learn.

Persistence and self-discipline are everything. The continual dripping of water will wear away a stone. If you keep working hard, you will achieve your goal. Things take time.

You were born for a reason. Find out what it is and do it.

These are just a few examples out of hundreds of answers given to me. I didn't include more in this book, because they were really the same messages couched in different words. In fact, after reading the hundreds of replies, I found that they boiled down to ten commandments. See if any of your teachers have tried to inspire you to live up to any or all of the following ideals.

1. Follow your dream.
2. Work hard. It pays off in the long run.
3. Use your potential to the fullest.
4. Treat people the way you wish to be treated.
5. Be diligent and persistent. Never give up.
6. Be responsible.
7. Use self-discipline.
8. Value an education. Learn as much as you can.
9. Be honest. Integrity is a much-respected quality.
10. You are a unique individual. Dare to be yourself.

Have I left any out? If so, please write to me at my P.O. box listed in the back of the book. I'd love to hear from you. I'd also like to hear about your favorite teacher.

-WHO ASKED THEM
TO CARE?-

Do any of the above messages sound familiar? If so, where did you hear them before? From your mother, father, aunt, uncle, grandparent, or religious leader? Of course you did. But why do teachers, who are not related to you and not responsible for your religious education, take the time and energy to try to get you to absorb these values? Isn't it true that your teacher is being paid to teach a subject, not a philosophy of life? If so, why is it that not one of the teachers interviewed had a message such as, "Study math and become an accountant" or "Learn your grammar because it is important to speak and write correctly"?

It seems clear that teachers feel responsible for your education in the broadest sense of that word: "To bring up from childhood, so as to form habits, manners, mental and physical aptitude." Though their pay is not affected one way or the other by whether your "habits and manners" are likely to help you to become fulfilled and happy or frustrated and miserable, they take upon themselves the tremendous burden of trying to instill in you the values that they believe will give you the best possible shot at a joyful existence. They do this only because they feel a sense of personal responsibility for your future, not because it is in any way a part of their job.

Of course, they realize that many of their students will not be interested in what they have to say. But nevertheless, they continue to do the best they can, day by day, pouring out their hearts to a "congregation" that they hope is listening and listening well.

-THE UNSUNG HEROES-

At the risk of sounding corny—please don't throw this book across the room—I have to tell you that teachers are the unsung heroes of our culture. A teacher looks at his or her profession not as a job but as a calling. Day by day, the teacher patiently plods away, trying to make a dent in the minds that will some day run the country.

Now that you know how we feel about teaching, perhaps you can forgive us if we get a little carried away sometimes. You see, we can't help ourselves, because we really care.

-AND BY THE WAY . . .-

It is not only the most wonderful teachers who have this kind of commitment to keeping and inspiring students. Most of the teachers discussed in chapters one through ten of this book as well—the very ones you call boors, burnouts, and martinets—care deeply about what happens to their students even if you don't much care for their manner of expressing that concern. When asked, they too admitted to having a special message that they try to get across day by day.

How can this be? As I keep emphasizing, teachers are human, so of course they will often have imperfections. Yes, even the "worst" teacher cares and has high ideals and goals for you.

What it boils down to is this: All teachers have a little "wonderful" in them—but some have more than others. Teachers are a dedicated, caring group of professionals who go the extra mile on a daily basis, stepping out of the narrowly defined domain of teacher, into the broader role of mother, father, aunt, uncle, friend, and at times, even psychologist.

-REMINDERS-

1. A wonderful teacher inspires you to use your potential to the fullest and to reach for your dream.

2. Teachers believe that they have the responsibility to influence not just your life in school but your life in the world beyond the classroom.

3. Teachers admit to preaching a continual sermon or message between the lines of their subject. This message boils down to a formula for a happy and successful life.

4. Can you think of a favorite teacher? How does he or she compare to the teachers discussed in this chapter? Write to me and let me know.

12

It's Your Life

After all is said and done, why should you bother to put forth the extra effort that is required to make the best of every class you're faced with in school? Why should you have to put in so much work just because the teacher is not what you expect?

The answer is obvious and inevitable. If you fail a course or get a low grade in it, it won't matter one bit that it was because your teacher was boring, unfair, or sarcastic. No one will write on your record card, "but it wasn't his fault. . . ." The fact is, if you're smart, you'll be mature about it and begin to consider the big picture. Put aside the immediate pleasure of telling the teacher off or running away from the situation by cutting the class, and instead take the challenge before you. Use your mind to figure out a way to turn the situation around so that it can work for you. Get your credit for that course, pass it with the highest mark possible, and be proud of yourself.

-A RUDE AWAKENING
IN COLLEGE-

It's a good idea to start using that self-discipline now, because in college, you won't have a choice. You'll be forced to use it or fail. One of the first lessons you will learn in your freshman year of college is that the teachers expect you to be self-motivated. Not only do they not check homework (and I mean never), but they don't usually bother with surprise quizzes or even spot checks.

If you participate in class discussions, great. If you don't, they simply forget that you exist and teach to the ones who appear to be listening and want to get involved. The only time college teachers evaluate you is when test or term-paper time rolls around, and that's once or twice a semester.

Where is all of the self-discipline suddenly going to come from? How will you be able not only to keep up with large amounts of unsupervised reading and studying, but also to attend classes in huge lecture halls where professors never take notice of your presence, drone on in a monotone for two solid hours during which you are expected to take detailed notes, never call on you in class unless you raise your hand, never get to know their students personally, and never have any idea of whether the students understand the subject matter until they take the final exam?

-ENJOY IT WHILE IT LASTS-

In college, you will discover that, for the most part, your professors share a common attitude: It's your life. It is then that you will realize how caring your high school teachers were—your math teacher who nagged you to do your homework, the English teacher who called your home, and the American history teacher, be he ever so boring, who gave a test every Monday. The difference between high school and college may make you feel lost for a while. Eventually you'll get used to the independence and the high expectations, and you'll no longer feel so threatened; but the sooner you start practicing some self-discipline, the easier it will be for you to adjust. So start now in order to avoid major culture shock in college. If you're not going to college, the same still applies, because self-discipline and hard work that will help other people succeed in college will help you succeed in your life, too.

In the meantime, consider yourself lucky that now, while you are still in high school, there are people who are willing to nag you, preach to you, and try to motivate you—teachers who take on a role that is far grater than what is required of them. Take advantage of what they have to offer while you can.

–LEARN TO RELY ON YOURSELF–

Wouldn't it be wonderful if you could have someone to rely on—someone who you knew wouldn't let you down? Well you can. That person can be yourself. The only way to make this happen is to take action in small steps. Every single act of will—of self-discipline—is a signal to you that you are in control of your life, that you can cause your life to go in one direction or another, that you can depend on yourself.

For example, every time you refuse to cut a class just because it's boring, you are sending yourself a message: "I can endure unpleasant situations in order to achieve a goal." And the next time you're faced with a challenge, you will believe that you can overcome that, too. In time, you will realize that you are responsible for your own life, and you will be happy about that, because you won't let yourself down. You can become your own best friend and ally.

–IT'S YOUR LIFE–

Right now, begin doing what you have to do not only to pass every course, but to get the highest mark possible. Using the suggestions in this book, take on the challenge. Accept the fact that it's your life, and even though your teachers may not be all they should be, or all you want them to be, when it comes down to it, you are the one who will have to pay the price if you just throw up your hands and say, "I can't take this." So instead of running away from the problem, attack it head on and let me know what happens.

You may write to me at the following address. Please enclose a stamped, self-addressed envelope if you wish a reply.

Dr. Joyce L. Vedral
P.O. Box A 433
Wantagh, NY 11793-0433

–BIBLIOGRAPHY–

Other books for teens by Joyce Vedral

I Dare You. A "How to Win Friends and Influence People" for teenagers. Motivates teens to overcome obstacles and achieve goals, and shows them how to use psychology in dealing with teachers, friends, bosses, etc., in order to make things run more smoothly.

My Parents Are Driving Me Crazy. Gives teenagers insight into the workings of the adult, specifically "parent," mind. Helps teens to become more loving, compassionate, and understanding of parents. Teens who have read the book say that it has totally changed their relationships with their parents.

I Can't Take It. A suicide prevention guide. This book shows teens how to deal with anger, rage, hate, fear, rejection, and other emotions that could potentially destroy their lives. Tells how to channel these emotions towards goals they can achieve instead of turning them inward. Many young adults have written that the words from this book have come back to them and helped them to go on when they were feeling down or even having suicidal thoughts.

The Opposite Sex Is Driving Me Crazy. Helps teenagers to understand why members of the opposite sex behave the way they do. The book is divided into halves: In the first part, girls answer favorite questions posed by boys; in the second, boys answer typical questions asked by girls. Topics such as jealousy and cheating, sex, money, time together and time apart, and turn-ons and turn-offs are covered. Teens are shown that they are not ''weird'' or ''rejects'' and are given ways to deal with even the most cruel behavior of the opposite sex, at the same time that they're encouraged to build full, rich lives for themselves so that even when a romance doesn't work out, life will still be worth living.

Boyfriends: Getting Them, Keeping Them, Living Without Them. Shows teenage girls how to attract and keep the attention of the guy she has in mind, and how to ''make the first move'' without seeming obvious. Gives insight into the insecurities of boys and shows girls what is really behind some of their angry words and deeds. Talks about how sex changes the relationship and deals with why boys sometimes break up with girls shortly after sex enters the relationship; also gives advice on what to do in such a situation. Helps girls to get over a broken heart, and to find ways to enjoy life even more after the break-up. Helps to build self-confidence and self-esteem.

You may order the books by calling 1-800-733-3000.

INDEX

ABOUT THE AUTHOR

Joyce Vedral, a Ph.D. in English Literature, teaches English at Julia Richman High School in New York City. She is also an adjunct professor in English at Pace University. She has written for *Seventeen* and *Parents*, and she is a regular contributor to *Muscle and Fitness* magazine. She is the author of *I Dare You*; *I Can't Take It Anymore*; *My Parents are Driving Me Crazy*; *The Opposite Sex Is Driving Me Crazy*; *My Teanager is Driving Me Crazy*, and *Boyfriends: Getting Them, Keeping them, Living Without Them*. She lives in Wantagh, Long Island, with her teenage daughter, Marthe.